THE QUESTION

OF BRUNO

ALEKSANDAR
HEMON

NAN A. TALESE
DOUBLEDAY
NEW YORK LONDON
TORONTO SYDNEY AUCKLAND

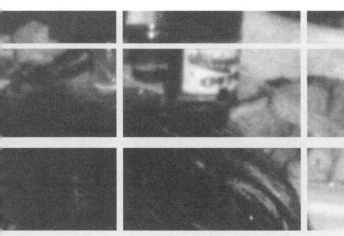

THE QUESTION
OF BRUNO

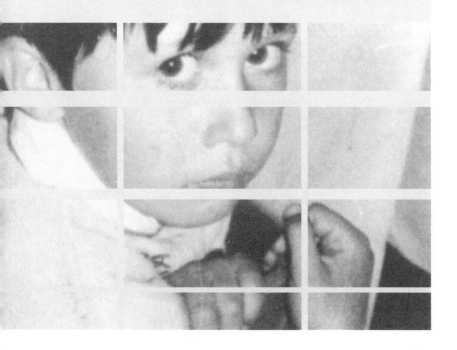

PUBLISHED BY NAN A. TALESE
an imprint of Doubleday
a division of Random House, Inc.
1540 Broadway, New York, New York 10036

DOUBLEDAY is a trademark of Doubleday,
a division of Random House, Inc.

Book design by Terry Karydes

Some of the stories in this book have appeared, in different form,
in the following publications: "Islands" in *Ploughshares* and *Best
American Short Stories 1999*, "The Life and Work of Alphonse
Kauders" in *TriQuarterly* and, in Serbo-Croatian, in *Best Yugoslav
Short Stories 1990*, "The Sorge Spy Ring" in *TriQuarterly*, "Ex-
change of Pleasant Words" in *Granta*, "A Coin" in *Chicago Re-
view*, and extracts from "Blind Jozef Pronek & Dead Souls" in *The
New Yorker* and *The Baffler*.

Library of Congress Cataloging-in-Publication Data
Hemon, Aleksandar, 1964–
The question of Bruno / Aleksandar Hemon.— 1st ed.
p.   cm.
Contents: The life and work of Alphonse Kauders—The Sorge
spy ring—The accordion—Exchange of pleasant words—
A coin—Blind Josef Pronek & dead souls—Imitation of life.
1. Sarajevo (Bosnia and Hercegovina)—Social life and customs—
Fiction. 2. Chicago (Ill.)—Social life and customs—Fiction.
3. Bosnian Americans—Illinois—Chicago—Fiction. I. Title.

PS3558.E479155 Q47 2000
813'.54—dc21   99-057519

ISBN 0-385-49923-X
Copyright © 2000 by Aleksandar Hemon
All Rights Reserved
Printed in the United States of America
May 2000
1   3   5   7   9   10   8   6   4   2
First Edition

FOR SARAJEVO

FOR MY WIFE

CONTENTS

ISLANDS

1

We got up at dawn, ignored the yolky sun, loaded our navy-blue Austin with suitcases and then drove straight to the coast, stopping only on the verge of Sarajevo, so I could pee. I sang communist songs the entire journey: songs about mournful mothers looking through graves for their dead sons; songs about the revolution, steaming and steely, like a locomotive; songs about striking miners burying their dead comrades. By the time we got to the coast, I had almost lost my voice.

2

We waited for the ship on a long stone pier, which burnt the soles of my feet, as soon as I took off my sandals. The air was sweltering, saturated with sea-ozone, exhaustion, and the smell of coconut sunscreen, coming from the German tourists, already red and shellacked, lined up for a photo at the end of the pier. We saw the thin stocking of smoke on the horizon-thread, then the ship itself, getting bigger, slightly slanted sideways, like a child's drawing. I had on a round straw hat with all the seven dwarves painted on it. It threw a short, dappled shadow over my face. I had to raise my head to look at the grown-ups. Otherwise, I would look at their gnarled knees, the spreading sweat stains on their shirts and sagging wrinkles of fat on their thighs. One of the Germans, an old, bony man, got down on his knees and puked over the pier edge. The vomit hit the surface and then dispersed in different directions, like children running away to hide from the seeker. Under the wave-throbbing, ochre and maroon, island of vomit, a school of aluminum fish gathered and nibbled it peevishly.

3

The ship was decrepit, with pealing steel stairs and thin leaves of rust that could cut your fingers on the handrails. The staircase wound upward like a twisted towel. "Welcome," said an unshaven man in a T-shirt picturing a boat with a smoke-snake, wobbling on the waves, and, above it, the sun with a U-smile and an umlaut of eyes. We sat on the upper deck and the ship leapt over humble waves, panting and belching. We passed a line of little islands, resembling car wrecks by the road, and I would ask my parents: "Is this Mljet?" and they would say: "No." From behind one of the petrified islands, shaven by a wildfire, a gust of waylaying wind attacked us, snatched the straw hat off my head and tossed it into the sea. I watched the hat teetering away, my hair pressed against my skull, like a helmet, and I understood that I would never, ever see it again. I wished to go back in time and hold on to my hat before the surreptitious whirlwind hit me in the face. The ship sped away from the hat and the hat was transformed into a beige stain on the snot-green sea. I began crying and sobbed myself to sleep. When I woke up the ship was docked and the island was Mljet.

4

Uncle Julius impressed a stern, moist kiss on my cheek—the corner of his mouth touched the corner of my mouth, leaving a dot of spit above my lip. But his lips were soft, like slugs, as if there was nothing behind to support them. As we walked away from the pier, he told us that he forgot his teeth at home, and then, so as to prove that he was telling us the truth, he grinned at me, showing me his pink gums with cinnabar scars. He reeked of pine cologne, but a whiff redolent of rot and decay escaped his insides and penetrated the fragrant cloud. I hid my face in my mother's skirt. I heard his snorting chuckle. "Can we please go back home!" I cried.

5

We walked up a dilapidated, sinuous road exuding heat. Uncle Julius's sandals clattered in a tranquilizing rhythm and I felt sleepy. There was a dense verdureless thicket alongside the road. Uncle Julius told us that there used to be so many poisonous snakes on Mljet that people used to walk in tall rubber boots all the time, even at home, and snakebites were as common as mosquito bites. Everybody used to know how to slice off the bitten piece of flesh in a split second, before the venom could spread. Snakes killed chickens and dogs. Once, he said, a snake was attracted by the scent of milk, so it curled up on a sleeping baby. And then someone heard of the mongoose, how it kills snakes with joy, and they sent a man to Africa and he brought a brood of mongooses and they let them loose on the island. There were so many snakes that it was like a paradise for them. You could walk for miles and hear nothing but the hissing of snakes and the shrieks of mongooses and the bustle and rustle in the thicket. But then the mongooses killed all the snakes and bred so much that the island became too small for them. Chickens started disappearing, cats also. There were rumors of rabid mongooses and some even talked about monster mongooses that were the result of paradisiacal inbreeding. Now they were trying to figure out how to get rid of mongooses. So that's how it is, he said, it's all one pest after another, like revolutions. Life is nothing if not a succession of evils, he said, and then stopped and took a pebble out of his left sandal. He showed the puny, gray pebble to us, as if holding irrefutable evidence that he was right.

6

He opened the gate and we walked through a small, orderly garden with stout tomato stalks like sentries alongside the path. His wife (he pointed her out to us) stood in the courtyard, her face like a loaf of bread with a small tubby potato in the middle, arms akimbo, her calves full of bruises and blood vessels on the verge of bursting, ankles swollen. She was barefoot, her big toes were crooked, taking a sudden turn, as if backing away in disgust from each other. She enveloped my head with her palms, twisted my head upward and then put her mouth over my mouth, leaving a thick layer of warm saliva, which I hastily wiped off with my shoulder. Aunt Lyudmila was her name.

7

I clambered, dragging a bag full of plastic beach toys, after my sprightly parents, up a concrete staircase on the side of the house, with sharp stair edges and pots of unconcerned flowers, like servants with candles, on the banister side.

8

The room was fragrant with lavender, mosquito-spray poison, and clean, freshly ironed bed sheets. There was an aerial picture of a winding island (Mljet, it said in the lower right corner) and a picture of Comrade Tito, smiling, black-and-white, on the opposite wall. Below the window, the floor was dotted with mosquitoes—with a large green-glittering fly or a bee, here and there—still stricken by the surprise. When I moved toward them, the whisp caused by my motion made them ripple away from me, as if retreating, wary of another surprise.

9

I lay on the bed, listening to the billowing-curtain flaps, looking at the picture of Mljet. There were two oblong lakes, touching each other, at the top end of the picture-island, and on one of those lakes there was another island.

10

I woke up and the night was rife with the cicada hum, perpetual as if it were the hum of the island engine. They were all sitting outside, around the table underneath the shroud of vine twisting up the lattice. There was a long-necked carafe, full of black wine, in the center of the table, like an axis. Uncle Julius was talking and they all laughed. He would bulge his eyes, lean forward; he would thrust his fist forward, then open it and the hand would have the index-finger pointed at the space between my mother and his wife; and then the hand would retract back into the fist, but the finger would reappear, tapping its tip against the table, as if telegraphing a message. He would, then, stop talking and withdraw back into the starting position, and he would just watch them as they laughed.

11

Uncle Julius spoke: "We brought beekeeping to Bosnia. Before the Ukrainians came, the natives kept their bees in mud-and-straw hives and when they wanted the honey they would just kill them all with sulfur. My grandfather had fifty beehives three years after coming to Bosnia. Before he died, he was sick for a long time. And the day he died, he asked to be taken to the bees and they took him there. He sat by the hives for hours, and wept and wept, and wept out a sea of tears, and then they put him back into his bed and an hour later he died."

"What did he die of?" Aunt Lyudmila asked.

"Dysentery. People used to die of that all the time. They'd just shit themselves to death."

12

I went down the stairs and announced my thirst. Aunt Lyudmila walked over to the dark corner on my right-hand side—suddenly the light was ablaze—and there was a concrete box with a large wooden lid. She took off the lid and grabbed a tin cup and shoved her arm into the square. I went to the water tank (for that's what it really was) and peeked over. I saw a white slug on the opposite wall. I could not tell whether it was moving upward or it was just frozen by our sudden presence. The dew on its back twinkled, and it looked like a severed tongue. I glanced at Aunt Lyudmila, but she didn't seem to have noticed anything. She offered me the cup, but I shook my head and refused to drink the water which, besides, seemed turbid.

So they brought me a slice of cold watermelon and I drowsily masticated it. "Look at yourself," Uncle Julius said. "You don't want to drink the water! What would you do if you were so thirsty that you were nearly crazy and having one thought only: water, water! and there's no water. How old are you?"

"Nine," my mother said.

13

Uncle Julius told us that when he was in the Arkhangelsk camp, Stalin and his parliament devised a law that said if you were repeatedly late for school or missed several days with no excuse, you would get six months to three years in a camp. So, suddenly, in 1943, the camp was full of children, only a little bit older than I was—twelve, fifteen years old. They didn't know what to do in the camp, so the criminals took the nicest-looking to their quarters and fed them and, you know (no, I didn't), abused them. So they were there. They died like flies, because it was cold, and they lost their warm clothing, they didn't know how to preserve or protect the scarce food and water they were allotted. Only the ones that had protectors were able to survive. And there was a boy named Vanyka:

gaunt, about twelve, blond, blue eyes. He survived by filching food from the weaker ones, by lending himself to different protectors and bribing guards. Once—I think he drank some vodka with the criminals—he started shouting: "Thank you, Vozhd, for my happy childhood!" At the top of his lungs: "Thank you, Stalin, for my happy childhood!" And they beat him with gun butts and took him away.

14

"Don't torture the boy with these stories. He won't be able to sleep ever again."

"No, let him hear, he should know."

15

Then they sent Uncle Julius to a different camp, and then to another one, and he didn't even know how much time or how many camps he passed through, and he found himself in Siberia. One spring, his job was to dig big graves in the thawing ground, take the dead to the grave on a large cart, and then stuff them into the grave. Fifty per grave was the prescribed amount. Sometimes he had to stamp on the top of the graveload to get more space and meet the plan. He had big, big boots. One day they told him that there was a dead man in solitary confinement, so he pushed his cart there and put the corpse on the cart, and as he was pushing, the corpse moaned: "Let me die! Let me die!" I was so scared I almost died, I fell down and he kept moaning: "Let me die! I don't want to live!" So I pushed the cart behind the barrack and I leaned over him.

He was emaciated and had no teeth and one of his ears was missing, but he had blue, blue eyes. It was Vanyka! He looked much older, oh my God! So I gave him a piece of bread that I had saved and told him that I remembered him and this is what he told me.

16

They took him away and mauled him for days and did all sorts of things to him. Then they moved him to another camp and he had problems there all the time, because he would speak out again, despite his better judgment. He knew how to steal from the weaker and there were still men who liked him. He won acclaim when he killed a marked person, some Jew, after losing a card game. He killed more. He did bad, bad things and learned how to survive, but he could never keep his snout shut. So they sent him to the island where they kept the worst of the worst. The nearest guard was on the shore fifty kilometers away. They let the inmates rob and kill each other like mad dogs. Once a month the guards would come in, leave the food and count the corpses and graves and go back to their barracks by the sea. So one day Vanyka and two others killed some other inmates, took their food and clothes and set out on foot toward the shore. It was a very, very cold winter—pines would crack like matches every day—so they thought they could walk over the frozen strait, if they avoided the guards. But they got lost and ran out of food and Vanyka and one of the other two agreed by exchanging glances to kill the third one. And they did and they ate his flesh, and they walked and walked and walked. Then Vanyka killed the other one and ate him. But the guards with dogs tracked him down and caught him and he ended up in solitary confinement here and he didn't know how long he had been there. All he wanted was to die and he'd smash his head against the walls and he'd try to choke himself with his tongue. He refused to eat, but they'd force him, if only to make him live longer and suffer more. "Let me die!" he cried and cried.

17

Uncle Julius fell reticent and no one dared to say anything. But I asked: "So what happened to him?"

"He was killed," he said, making a motion with his hand, as if thrusting me aside, out of his sight.

18

I woke up and didn't know where I was or who I was, but then I saw the photo of Mljet and I recognized it. I got up, out of my nonbeing, and stepped into the inchoate day. It was pur-blindingly bright, but I could hear the din of the distant beach: bashful whisper of waves, echoes of sourceless music, warbling of boat motors, shrieks of children, syncopated splashing of oars. Bees levitated over the staircase flowers and I passed them cautiously. There was breakfast on the table in the net-like shadow of the vines: a plate with smoldering soggy eggs, a cup with a stream of steam rushing upward, and seven slices of bread, on a mirroring steel tray, leaning on each other like fallen dominoes. There was no one around, apart from shad-ows stretching on the courtyard stone pavement. I sat down and stirred my white coffee. There was a dead bee in the whirl and it kept revolving on its back, slower and slower, until it came to a reluctant stop.

19

After breakfast, we would go down a dirt path resembling a long burrow in the shrub. I'd carry my blue-and-white Nivea inflatable ball and sometimes I would inadvertently drop it and it would bounce ahead of us, in slow motion. I'd hear a bustle in the thicket—a snake, perhaps. But then there would be more bustling and I'd imagine a mongoose killing the snake, the whole bloody battle, the writhing snake entangled with the mongoose trying to bite off its head, just the way I saw it on TV, on *Survival.* I'd wait for my parents, for I didn't know what sort of feeling a fierce mongoose would have toward a curious boy—would it, perhaps, want to bite his head off?

20

We'd get to the gravel beach, near the dam dividing the two lakes. I'd have to sit on the prostrate towel for a while before I would be allowed to swim. On the left, there would usually be an old man, his skin puckered here and there, a spy novel over his face, white hair bristling meekly on his chest, his belly ascending and descending nearly imperceptibly, with a large metallic-green fly on the brim of his navel. On our right, two symmetrical old men, with straw hats and baggy trunks, would play chess in serene silence, with their doughy breasts overlooking the board. There would be three children a little farther away. They would sit on their towel, gathered around a woman, probably their mother, who would distribute tomatoes and slices of bread with a layer of sallow spread on them. The children would all simultaneously bite into their slices and their tomatoes, and then chew vigorously. The tomato slime would drip down their chins, they would be seemingly unperturbed, but when they were done eating, the mother would wipe their recalcitrant faces with a stained white rag.

21

Finally, my parents would tell me I could swim and I'd totter over the painful gravel and enter the shallows. I would see throbbing jellyfish floating by. The rocks at the bottom were covered with slimy lichen. I'd hesitantly dive and the shock of coldness would make me feel present in my own body—I'd be aware that my skin was the border between the world and me. Then I'd stand up, the quivering lake up to my nipples, and I'd wave to my parents and they'd shout: "Five more minutes!"

22

Sometimes I'd see fish in pellucid water, gliding along the bottom. Once I saw a school of fish that looked like miniature swordfish, with silver bellies and pointed needle-noses. They were all moving as one and then they stopped before me, and hundreds of little wide-open eyes stared at me in dreadful surprise. Then I blinked and they flitted away.

23

We walked up the path as the sun was setting. Everything attained a brazen shade and, now and then, there would be a thin gilded beam, like a spear, sticking out of the ground. Cicadas were revving and the warmth of the ground enhanced the fragrance of dry pine needles on the path. I entered the stretch of the path that had been in the shadow of the tall pines for a while, and the sudden coolness made me conscious of how hot my shoulders felt. I pressed my thumb firmly against my shoulder and, when I lifted it, a pallid blot appeared, then it slowly shrank, back into the ruddiness.

24

There was a man holding a German shepherd on a leash, much of which was coiled around his hand. The shepherd was attempting to jump at a mongoose backed against a short ruin of a stone wall. As the dog's jaw snapped a breath away from the mongoose's snout, the man pulled the dog back. The mongoose's hair bristled up, and it grinned to show its teeth, appearing dangerous, but I knew it was just madly scared. The eyes had a red glow, akin to the glow that people who glanced at the flashbulb have on bad color photos. The dog was growling and barking and I saw the pink-and-brown gums and the bloodthirsty saliva running down the sides of the jaw. Then the man let the dog go and there was, for just a moment, hissing and wheezing, growling and shrieking. The man yanked the dog back and the mongoose lay on its back, showing its teeth in a useless scowl, the paws spread, as if showing it was harmless now, and the eyes were wide open, the irises stretched to the edge of the pupils, flabbergasted. There was a hole in its chest—the dog seemed to have bitten off a part of it—and I saw the heart, like a tiny tomato, pulsating, as if hiccuping, slower and slower, with slightly longer moments between the throbs, and it simply stopped.

25

As we walked through the dusk, my sandals would fill with pine needles and I would have to stop to take them out. Thousands of fireflies floated in the shrubs, lighting and vanishing, as if they were hidden fairy-photographers with flashbulbs, taking our snapshots. "Are you hungry?" my mother asked.

26

We would sit under the cloak of vines, with a rotund jar of limpid honey and a plate of pickles. Uncle Julius would dip a pickle into the honey and several bees would peel themselves off the jar and hover above the table. I would dip my finger and try to get it to my lips before the thinning thread of honey dripped on my naked thighs, but I would never make it.

Sometimes, around lunch time, Uncle Julius would take me to his apiary. He would put on a white overall and a white hat with a veil falling down on his chest, so he looked like a bride. He would light a torn rag and order me to hold it, so as to repel the bees. He would tell me to be absolutely silent and not to move and not to blink. I'd peek from behind his back, my hand with the smoldering rag stretching out. He would take the lid off a beehive, carefully, as if he were afraid of awakening the island, and the buzz would rise like a cloud of dust and linger around us. He would scrape off the wax between the frames and then take them out, one by one, and show them to me. I'd see the molasses of bees fidgeting. "They work all the time," he'd whisper. "They never stop." I'd be frightened by the possibility of being stung, even though he told me that the bees would not attack me if I pretended not to exist. The fear would swell, and the more I'd think about it, the more unbearable the unease would be. Eventually, I'd break down and run back to the house, get on the stairs, from where I'd see him, remote, immobile—apart from the slow, wise motions of his apt hands. I'd watch him, as if he were projected on a screen of olive trees and aisles of beehives, then he'd turn to me and I could discern a peculiar, tranquil smile behind the veil.

27

Mother and Father were sitting at the stern, with their feet in tepid bilge water, Uncle Julius was rowing, and I was sitting at the prow, my feet dangling overboard. The surface of the lake would ascend with an inconspicuous wave and my feet would delve into the coolness of menthol-green water. With the adaggio of oars, creaking and splashing, we glissaded toward the lake island. There was a dun stone building, with small drawn-in windows, and an array of crooked olive trees in front of it. Uncle Julius steered the scow toward a short desolate pier. I slipped stepping out, but Uncle Julius grabbed my hand and

I hung for a moment over the throbbing lake with a sodden loaf of bread and an ardently smiling woman on a magazine page, stuck to the surface like an ice floe.

28

"These lakes," Uncle Julius said, "used to be a pirate haven in the sixteenth century. They'd hoard the loot and bring hostages here and kill them and torture them—in this very building—if they didn't get the ransom. They say that this place is still haunted by the ghosts of three children they hung on meat hooks because their parents didn't pay the ransom. Then this was a nunnery and some people used to believe that even the nuns were not nuns but witches. Then it was a German prison. And now, mind you, it's a hotel, but there are hardly any tourists ever."

29

We walked into the sonorous chill of a large stone-walled hall. There was a reception desk, but nobody behind it, and a smiling Tito-picture over the numbered cubbyhole shelf. Then we walked through a long tunnel and then through a low door, so everyone but me had to bow their heads, then we were in a cubicle-like windowless room ("This used to be a nun cell," Uncle Julius whispered), then we entered the eatery (they had to bend their knees and bow their heads, as if genuflecting, again) with long wooden tables and, on them, two parallel rows of plates and utensils. We sat there waiting for the waiter. There was a Popsicle-yellow lizard, as big as a new pencil, on the stone wall behind Uncle Julius's back. It looked at us with an unblinking marble eye, apparently perplexed, and then it scurried upward, toward an obscure window.

30

This was what Uncle Julius told us:

"When I was a young student in Moscow, in the thirties, I saw the oldest man in the world. I was in a biology class, it was in a gigantic amphitheater, hundreds of rows, thousands of students. They brought in an old man who couldn't walk, so two comrades carried him and he had his arms over their shoulders. His feet were dangling between them, but he was all curled up like a baby. They said he was a hundred and fifty-eight years old and from somewhere in the Caucasus. They put him sideways on the desk and he started crying like a baby, so they gave him a stuffed toy—a cat, I think, but I can't be certain, because I was sitting all the way up in one of the last aisles. I was looking at him as if through the wrong side of a telescope. And the teacher told us that the old man cried all the time, ate only liquid foods, and couldn't bear being separated from his favorite toy. The teacher said that he slept a lot, didn't know his name and had no memories. He could say only a couple of words, like water, poo-poo and such. I figured out then that life is a circle, you get back right where you started if you get to be a hundred and fifty-eight years old. It's like a dog chasing its own tail, all is for naught. We live and live, and in the end we're just like this boy [he pointed at me], knowing nothing, remembering nothing. You might as well stop living now, my son. You might just as well stop, for nothing will change."

31

When I woke up, after a night of unsettling dreams, the suitcases were agape and my parents were packing them with
wrinkled underwear and shirts. Uncle Julius came up with a
jar of honey as big as my head and gave it to my father. He
looked at the photo of Mljet and then put the tip of his finger
at the point in the upper-right corner, near the twin lakes,
which looked like gazing eyes. "We are here," he said.

32

The sun had not risen yet from behind the hill, so there were
no shadows and everything looked muffled, as if under a sheet
of fine gauze. We walked down the narrow road and the asphalt was cold and moist. We passed a man carrying a cluster
of dead fish, with the hooks in their carmine gills. He said:
"Good morning!" and smiled.

We waited at the pier. A shabby boat, with paint falling off
and *Pirate* written in pale letters on the prow, was heading,
coughing, toward the open sea. A man with an anchor tattooed
on his right arm was standing at the rudder. He had a torn red-
and-black flannel shirt, black soccer shorts, and no shoes—his
feet were bloated and filthy. He was looking straight ahead toward the ferry that was coming into the harbor. The ferry
slowed down to the point of hesitant floating, and then it
dropped down its entrance door, like a castle bridge, with a
harsh peal. It was a different ship than the ship we had come

on, but the same man with the hobbling-boat shirt said: "Welcome!" again, and smiled, as if recognizing us.

We passed the same islands. They were like heavy, moulded loaves of bread, dropped behind a gigantic ship. On one of the islands, and we passed it close by, there was a herd of goats. They looked at us mildly confounded, and then, one by one, lost interest and returned to grazing. A man with a camera, probably a German tourist, took a picture of the goats, and then gave the camera to his speckle-faced, blue-eyed son. The boy pointed the camera toward the sun, but the man jokingly admonished him, turning him, and the camera, toward us, while we grinned at him, helpless.

33

It took us only four hours to get home from the coast and I slept the whole time, oblivious to the heat, until we reached Sarajevo. When we got home, the shriveled plants and flowers were in the midst of the setting-sun orange spill. All the plants had withered, because the neighbor who was supposed to water them died of a sudden heart attack. The cat, having not been fed for more than a week, was emaciated and nearly mad with hunger. I would call her, but she wouldn't come to me; she would just look at me with irreversible hatred.

THE LIFE AND WORK

OF

ALPHONSE KAUDERS

Alphonse Kauders is the creator of *The Forestry Bibliography, 1900–1948*, published by the Engineers and Technicians Association, in Zagreb, 1949. This is a special bibliography related to forestry. The material is classified into seventy-three groups and encompasses 8,800 articles and theses. Bibliographical units are not numbered. The creator of *The Forestry Bibliography* was the first to catalog the entire forest matter in a single piece of work. The work has been viewed as influential.

Alphonse Kauders had a dog by the name of Rex, whose whelp, in the course of time, he gave to Josip B. Tito.

Alphonse Kauders had a mysterious prostate illness and, in the course of time, he said: "Strange are the ways of urine."

Alphonse Kauders said to Rosa Luxemburg: "Let me penetrate a little bit, just a bit, I'll be careful."

Alphonse Kauders said: "And what if I am still here."

Alphonse Kauders was the only son of his father, a teacher. He was locked up in a lunatic asylum, having attempted to molest seven seven-year-old girls at the same time. Father, a teacher.

Alphonse Kauders said to Dr. Joseph Goebbels: "Writing is a useless endeavor. It is as though we sign every molecule of gas, say, of air, which—as we all know—cannot be seen. Yet, signed gas, or air, is easier to inhale."

Dr. Joseph Goebbels said: "Well, listen, that differs from a gas to a gas."

Alphonse Kauders was the owner of the revolver used to assassinate King Alexander.

One of Alphonse Kauders's seven wives had a tumor as big as a three-year-old child.

Alphonse Kauders said: "People are so ugly that they should be liberated from the obligation to have photos in their identity cards. Or, at least, in their Party cards."

Alphonse Kauders desired, passionately, to create a bibliography of pornographic literature. He held in his head 3,700 pornographic books. Plus magazines.

Richard Sorge, talking about the winds of Alphonse Kauders, said: "They sounded like sobs, sheer heartrending sorrow, which, resembling waves, emerged from the depths of one's soul, and, then, broke down, someplace high, high above."

Alphonse Kauders, in the course of time, had to crawl on all fours for seven days, for his penis had been stung by seventy-seven bees.

Alphonse Kauders owned complete lists of highly promiscuous women in Moscow, Berlin, Marseilles, Belgrade, and Munich.

Alphonse Kauders was a Virgin in his horoscope. And in his horoscope only.

Alphonse Kauders never, never wore or carried a watch.

There are records suggesting that the five-year-old Alphonse Kauders amazed his mother by making "systematic order" in the house pantry.

Alphonse Kauders said to Adolf Hitler, in Munich, as they were guzzling down their seventh mug of beer: "God, mine is always hard when it is needed. And it is always needed."

Alphonse Kauders:
a)   hated forests
b)   loved to watch fires
These proclivities were happily united in his notorious obsession with forest fires, which he would watch, with great pleasure, whenever he had a chance.

Josip B. Tito, talking about the winds of Alphonse Kauders, said: "They sounded like all the sirens of Moscow on May 1, the International Labor Day."

Alphonse Kauders impregnated Eva Braun, and she, in the course of time, delivered a child. But after Adolf Hitler began establishing new order and discipline and seducing Eva Braun, she, intoxicated by the Führer's virility, sent the child to a concentration camp, forcing herself to believe it was only for the summer.

Alphonse Kauders hated horses. Oh, how Alphonse Kauders hated horses.

Alphonse Kauders, in the course of time, truly believed that man created himself in the process of history.

Alphonse Kauders stood behind Gavrilo Princip, whispering—as urine was streaming down Gavrilo's thigh, as Gavrilo's sweating hand, holding a weighty revolver, was trembling in his pocket—Alphonse Kauders whispered: "Shoot, brother, what kind of a Serb are you?"

Alphonse Kauders described his relationship with Rex: "We, living in fear, hate each other."

There are records that Alphonse Kauders spent some years in a juvenile delinquents' home, having set seven forest fires in a single week.

Alphonse Kauders said: "I hate people, almost as much as horses, because there are always too many of them around, and because they kill bees, and because they fart and stink, and because they always come up with something, and it is the worst when they come up with irksome revolutions."

Alphonse Kauders wrote to Richard Sorge: "I cannot speak. Things around me do not speak. Still, dead, like rocks in a stream, they do not move, they have no meaning, they are just barely present. I stare at them, I beg them to tell me something, anything, to make me name them. I beg them to exist—they only buzz in the darkness, like a radio without a program, like an empty city, they want to say nothing. Nothing. I cannot stand the pressure of silence, even sounds are motionless. I cannot speak, words mean nothing to me. At times, my Rex knows more than I do. Much more. God bless him, he is silent."

Alphonse Kauders knew by heart the first fifty pages of the Berlin phone book.

Alphonse Kauders was the first to tell Joseph V. Stalin: "No!"

Stalin asked him: "Do you have a watch, Comrade Kauders?" and Alphonse Kauders said: "No!"

Alphonse Kauders, in the course of time, told the following: "In our party, there are two main factions: the Maniacs and the Killers. The Maniacs are losing their minds, the Killers are killing. Naturally, in neither of these two factions is there any women. Women are gathered in the faction called the Women. Chiefly, they serve as an excuse for bloody fights between the Maniacs and the Killers. The Maniacs are the better soccer team, but the Killers can do wonders with knives, like nobody else in this modern world of ours."

Alphonse Kauders had gonorrhea seven times and syphilis only once.

Alphonse Kauders does not exist in the *Encyclopedia of the USSR.* Then again, he does not exist in the *Encyclopedia of Yugoslavia.*

Alphonse Kauders said: "I am myself, everything else is stories."

Dr. Joseph Goebbels, talking about the winds of Alphonse Kauders, said: "They were akin to the wail of an everlastingly solitary siren, sorrow in the purest of forms."

One of the seven wives of Alphonse Kauders had a short leg. Then again, the other leg was long. The arms were, more or less, of the same length.

In the Archives of the USSR, there is a manuscript which is believed to have originated from Alphonse Kauders:
"1)   shoot under the tongue (?);
2)   symbolism (?); death on the ground (?); in the forest (??); by an anthill (?); by a beehive;
3)   take only one bullet;
4)   the sentence: I shall be reborn if this bullet fails, and I hope it won't;
5)   lie down, so all the blood flows into the head;
6)   burn all manuscripts => possibility of someone thinking they were worth something;
7)   invent some love (?);
8)   the sentence: I blame nobody, especially not Her (?);
9)   tidy up the room;
10)   write to Stalin: Koba, why did you need my death?
11)   take a bottle of water with me;
12)   avoid talking until the certain date."

One of Alphonse Kauders's seven best men was Richard Sorge.

Alphonse Kauders regularly subscribed to all the pornographic magazines of Europe.

Alphonse Kauders removed his own appendix in Siberia, and he probably would have died, had he not been transferred to the camp hospital at the very last moment. And that was only because he had informed on a bandit in the bed next to his for secretly praying at night.

Alphonse Kauders said to Eva Braun: "Money isn't everything. There is some gold too."

Alphonse Kauders was a fanatic beekeeper. In the course of his life, he led fierce and merciless battles against parasitic lice that ruthlessly exploit bees, and are known as "varoa."

Alphonse Kauders said: "The most beautiful fire (not being a forest one) I have ever seen, was when the Reichstag was ablaze."

The very idea of creating Alphonse Kauders occurred for the first time to his (future) mother. She said to the (future) father of Alphonse Kauders: "Let's make passionate love and create Alphonse Kauders."

Father said: "All right. But let's watch some, you know, pictures."

Alphonse Kauders was a member of seven libraries, of seven apicultural societies, of seven communist parties and of a national-socialist one.

Alphonse Kauders told the following: "In elementary school, I attracted attention by stuffing my fist into my mouth. Girls from other classes would rush in droves to see me stuff my fist into my mouth. My father, a teacher, glowed with a bliss, seeing all those girls swarming around me. Once, a girl that I wished to make love to approached me. And I was so excited that I tried to shove both of my fists into my mouth. I sacrificed my two front teeth for my passion. Ever since I have been noticed for my insanity. This strange event probably determined the course of my life. Ever since I haven't talked."

On one copy of *The Forestry Bibliography, 1900–1948*, kept in Zagreb, there is the following handwritten remark: "Since the day I was born, I have been waiting for the Judgment Day. And the Judgment Day is never coming. And, as I live, it is becoming all too clear to me. I was born after the Judgment Day."

Alphonse Kauders told the following: "When Rex and I had a fight, and that happened almost every day, he would stray and would be gone for days. And he would tell me nothing. Except once. He said: 'The stray-dog shelter is full of spies.' "

On the eve of World War II, in Berlin, Alphonse Kauders said to Ivo Andric: "A firm system still exists only in the minds of madmen. In other people's minds, there's nothing but chaos, as well as around them. Perhaps art is one of the last pockets of resistance to chaos. And then again, maybe it isn't. Who the hell cares?"

On the eve of World War I, Alphonse Kauders said to Archduke Franz Ferdinand's pregnant wife: "Let me penetrate a little bit, just a little, I'll be careful."

On one of Alphonse Kauders's seven tombs, it is written: "I have vanished and I have appeared. Now, I am here. I shall disappear and I shall return. And then, again, I shall be here. Everything is so simple. All one needs is courage."

Alphonse Kauders wrote to one of his seven wives letters "full of filthy details and sick pornographic fantasies." Stalin forbade such letters to be sent by Soviet mail, because "among those who open and read letters there are many tame, timid family people." So then Alphonse Kauders sent his letters through reliable couriers.

Alphonse Kauders said: "I—I am not a human being. I—I am Alphonse Kauders."

Alphonse Kauders said to Richard Sorge: "I doubt there exists an emptiness greater than that of empty streets. Therefore, it is better to have some tanks or bodies on the streets, if nothing else is possible. Because Anything is better than Nothing."

Alphonse Kauders, in the course of time, put a revolver on Gavrilo Princip's temple, for he had burned a bee with his cigarette.

Alphonse Kauders, in the course of time, said to Stalin: "Koba, if you shoot Bukharin ever again, we shall have an argument." And Bukharin was shot only once.

Alphonse Kauders said to Eva Braun—in bed, after seven mutual, consecutive orgasms, four of which had gone into the annals—Alphonse Kauders said to Eva Braun: "One should find a way of forbidding people to talk, especially to talk to each other. People should be forbidden to wear watches. Anything should be done with people."

It is widely believed that the little-known pornographic work *Seven Sweet Little Girls*, signed by pseudonym, was written by Alphonse Kauders.

Alphonse Kauders told, in the course of time, about the first days of the Revolution: "We killed all mad horses. We set empty houses on fire. We saw soldiers weeping. Crowds gushed out of prisons. Everybody was scared. And we had nothing but a bad feeling."

Albeit Alphonse Kauders hated folk from the depths of his soul, almost as much as he hated horses (Good God, how Alphonse Kauders hated horses!), he was the creator of a folk proverb: "Never a bee from a mare."

Joseph V. Stalin, talking about the winds of Alphonse Kauders, said: "Many a time, in the course of our Central Committee sessions, Comrade Kauders would, well, cut a wind, and a few moments later, all comrades would be helplessly crying. Including myself, as well."

Alphonse Kauders owned the revolver used to murder Lola, a twelve-year-old prostitute from Marseilles.

Ivo Andric, talking about Alphonse Kauders, said: "His insides were removed by a secret operation. All that remained was a sheath of skin, within which he safely dreamt of a bibliography of pornographic literature."

Alphonse Kauders spent the night between April 5 and April 6, 1941, on the slopes of Avala, waiting to see Belgrade in flames.

Alphonse Kauders killed his dog Rex with gas after Rex had tried to slaughter him in his sleep because Alphonse Kauders had set mousetraps all over their place to take revenge on Rex for having pissed on his new, pristine uniform.

Alphonse Kauders, in the course of time, was engaged in painting. The only painting that has been preserved, oil on canvas, is called *The Class Roots of Tattooing* and is kept in the National Museum in Helsinki.

Alphonse Kauders said to Josip B. Tito: "A few days, or years, hell, ago, I noticed that a tree under the window in one of my seven rooms had grown some ten goddamn meters. There aren't many people who notice trees growing at all. And those who do are likely to be lumberjacks."

Gavrilo Princip, talking about the winds of Alphonse Kauders, said: "They sounded like this: Pffffffuuummmiiuu-jmmsghhhss."

Alphonse Kauders had two legal sons and two legal daughters. The rest were illegal. One son was shot as a war criminal in Madona, Lithuania; the other was a distinguished member of the Australian national cricket team. One daughter was an interpreter at the Yalta conference; the other discovered, in the Amazon rain forests, a hitherto unknown species of an insect resembling the bee, labeled eventually Virgo Kauders.

Alphonse Kauders said: "Literature has nothing human in itself. Nor in myself."

Alphonse Kauders never finished work on the bibliography of pornographic literature.

NOTES

J. B. TITO was the Yugoslav communist leader for thirty-five long years. My childhood was saturated with histories of his just enterprises. My favorite one has always been the one in which he, at the age of twelve, found a whole, cooked pig's head in the house pantry, hoarded for Christmas, and, without telling his brothers and sisters, gorged himself with it on his own—an ominous act for a future communist head of a state. He was sick for days afterward (fat overdose), and was additionally punished by being banned from the Christmas dinner. Later on, he lost interest in Christmas, but never lost passion for pigs and heads.

ROSA LUXEMBURG was a German communist who attempted, with Karl Liebknecht, a socialist revolution in Germany after the end of World War I, and then withered with it. Rosa Luxemburg was a terribly nice name for a revolutionary.

KING ALEXANDER was a Yugoslav king and was assassinated in Marseilles, in 1934, by a Macedonian nationalist, with a generous support of Croatian fascists. Rickety propaganda machinery of the first Yugoslavia sermonized that his last words were: "Take care of my Yugoslavia." The likely truth, however, was that he gobbled and bolted his own blood, while a sweaty French secret policeman was protecting, with his own body, Alexander's ex-body, corpse-to-be. I always thought that the fact that an Alexander was assassinated by a Macedonian was as close as you can get to a nice touch in a farce.

RICHARD SORGE was a Soviet spy in Tokyo, undercover as a journalist, eventually becoming a press attaché in the German embassy. He informed Stalin that Hitler was going to attack the Motherland, but Stalin trusted Hitler and disregarded the information. The first time I read about Sorge I was ten and, not even having reached the end of the book, decided to become a spy. At the age of sixteen, I wrote a poem about Sorge entitled *The Loneliest Man in the World*. The first verse: "Tokyo is breathing and I am not."

GAVRILO PRINCIP was the young Serb who assassinated the Austrian Archduke Franz Ferdinand Habsburg and Sophia, his pregnant wife, thus effectively commencing World War I. He was eighteen at the time (I think) and had the first scrub over his thin lip and dark ripples around his eyes. He was incarcerated for life, which lasted only a few more years, and died of tuberculosis, blessed by repeated beatings, in an obscure imperial prison. In Sarajevo, by the Latin Bridge, at the corner from which he sent those historical bullets into the fetus's brain, his footprints were immortalized in concrete (left foot W-E, right foot SE-NW). When I was a little boy, I imagined him waiting for the Archduke's coach, waiting to change the course of history, stuck up to his ankles in wet concrete. When I was sixteen, my feet fit perfectly into his feet's tombs.

THE ENCYCLOPEDIA OF THE USSR is a book whose different editions are innumerable and often obscure. Historical characters (like Stalin's Secret Police chiefs) would be praised in one edition and then would be vanished in another. There are countries whose precious minerals (with annual production in parentheses) would be minutely listed by the encyclopedia's sanguine world map, and in another edition they would be swallowed by an ocean, much like Atlantis, without the bubble-burps ever reaching the surface of the map world. This great book teaches us how the verisimilitude of fiction is achieved by the exactness of the detail.

THE ENCYCLOPEDIA OF YUGOSLAVIA, on the other hand, was never even close to being entirely published, because of so many conflicting histories involved, so there really isn't any encyclopedic Yugoslavia, which by a snide turn of history, couldn't matter less, since Yugoslavia is not much of a country anymore.

NIKOLAI BUKHARIN, dubbed by Lenin "the darling of the Party," was a member of the Politburo and probably the main Soviet ideologue (save the great Stalin) in the thirties, for which he was rewarded with an accusation of spying, simultaneously, for the United States, Great Britain, France, and Germany. No one was surprised, but everyone was terrified when he was sentenced to death, for that was the beginning of one of Stalin's greatest purges. From his death cell, he sent a letter to Stalin, beginning with the words: "Koba, why did you need my death?", which Stalin is believed to have kept in his desk drawer for a long time. Bukharin voluntarily cooperated with his inquisitors and refused to be used as the martyr of Stalin's tyranny. If he is in a Dantesque inferno, he'll eternally bang his porcine head against the walls of hell's pantry.

IVO ANDRIC, a Bosnian, was the only Yugoslav author who has ever been awarded the Nobel Prize. In 1941, he worked in the Yugoslav embassy in Berlin, and helped organize trysts of cringing Yugoslav politicians with Hitler. He was a gentleman and wrote novels about the ways people are entangled with history. At the acceptance ceremony, he talked about the importance of bridges. In his youth, he was involved in organizing the Archduke's assassination.

On APRIL 6, 1941, at dawn, Belgrade was relentlessly bombed by the Luftwaffe. That was the beginning of the German attack on the Kingdom of Yugoslavia, which lasted for eleven more hapless days.

AVALA is a breast-like mountain near Belgrade, with the tomb-tumor for the Unknown Serbian Soldier, built after World War I.

THE YALTA CONFERENCE brought together Churchill, Roosevelt, and Stalin. The end of the war was in sight and they appeared to be the victors ("I'd like some Germany.") When I was thirteen, I saw a photo of those three great men in Yalta, sitting in three wicker chairs, against the background of standing people whose names were as insignificant as their deeds. The three heads of the free world had something like a dim grin on their round faces, as though they had done a good, hard work ("Have some Germany.") When I was thirteen, I thought that the picture was taken right after their lunch, because—as my father claimed—right after lunch is the best time, for people are "full and happy." I thought that behind their dim grins they were trying to get out last bits of food from between their teeth. They gaze at me, full of borscht, sweet Crimean wine, and plans for the world. Within a few moments Churchill will be asleep, and I'll be old, lacking significance, but not memories.

Now keep reading the book.

THE SORGE

SPY RING

HISTORY, a description or recital of things as they are, or have been, in a continued orderly narration of the principal facts and circumstances thereof. History, with regard to its subject, is divided into the History of Nature and the History of Actions. The History of Actions is a continued relation of a series of memorable events.

—ENCYCLOPAEDIA BRITANNICA
first edition (1769–1771)

The book was auburn, with black slanted letters on the spine reading "Spies of WWII," and, impressed onto the front cover, black letters, tiny trenches, with golden brims, reading: *The Greatest Spies of World War Two*. The book was big and weighty. I'd put it on my knees, but then its weight would spread my legs and the book would close itself and slip to the floor. And I'd lie on my belly and rest my head on the scaffold of my hands and read. When my elbows would begin to ache, I'd recline my cheek on the thicker half of the book, incline the other half, feeling the sticky moisture connecting my cheek and a spy's face, secrets of WWII just inches away from my absorbing pupils.

There were lots of black-and-white pictures: a five-man column—surrounded by soldiers pointing rifles—with their hands on the napes of their necks; when I would narrow my eyes, they'd look like black-and-white butterflies; the head of a chubby member of the *Rote Kappelle*,[1] with an asymmetrical face: nose slightly on the left side, right eye hardly opened and

---

[1] It seems that the *Rote Kapelle* network initially sent the information that German forces were going to attack the Soviet Union. Since the Ribbentrop-Molotov pact was considered to be valid and the source of the information was unclear, Moscow virtually ignored it. But when Sorge sent the confirmation from Tokyo, the information was passed on to the great Stalin himself. He, however, disregarded it and decided to trust Hitler and the Ribbentrop-Molotov pact. Sorge's report from Tokyo on German intentions was filed under the heading "Doubtful and Misleading Information."

seemingly asleep, mouth kept shut with effort, as if there was a spring of blood behind the feeble lips—I just knew from his face that his hands (swollen wrists, bloody, burning trenches under the cuffs) were handcuffed; a picture of General Montgomery standing, arms akimbo, turned sideways, looking at the upper-left corner of the page, with the timeless beret parallel with his gaze: General Montgomery's doppelganger, just the head, look-ing at me with odd pensiveness, as if painfully aware that he could never be General Montgomery; a row of blindfolded peo-ple in white in front of the ready firing squad and a smiling offi-cer, his right arm raised, pointing at the upper-right corner of the picture. And, near the end, there was Sorge—"at the outset of his mission in Japan"[2]—framed by a door behind his back, standing legs apart (left foot NW, right foot NE) in a dark trench-coat, one hand pocketed, the other somewhat clenched, holding

----

[2] Sorge flew from Berlin to Yokohama on Junker's first commercial flight from Germany to Japan, with brief stops in New York and Vancouver. Be-sides the flight log of Flight 1995, kept in the Museum of German Aviation in Frankfurt, there are no records of this historical endeavor. There is no list of passengers, but it is almost certain that the flight was almost full. It seems that the passengers were cosmopolitan, and that the flight was tumultuous ("Winds over the Pacific were just horrid!"); that something was wrong with the heating system, so the passengers were freezing even with mirac-ulously retrieved fur hats and leather gloves; that no one else slept on the flight; that the food was edible, but for some reason there was no water so they all drank champagne (courtesy of Junker); that the plane almost went down in the middle of the night, somewhere over the Pacific; that first men, then women, disgorged themselves all over the aircraft and the vomit froze on the floor; that Sorge briefly befriended a certain Mary Kinzie, an Amer-ican poetess, which did not go unnoticed by New York gossip-scribes. On September 9, 1933, in the early afternoon, Sorge and his shadowy co-pas-sengers arrived at the Yokohama airport, reeking of vomit, emptied of

a purse or a camera case; and his head: fiendish ears, large and
ill-shaped; lips shut tight, as if his teeth were biting the inside of
his lower lip; the wide base triangle of his nose, its top angle connected, by two deep furrows, with two dark dots in the corners of
his mouth; lightless twin-holes, at the bottom of which were his
eyes; and the black-inked helmet of hair.

The picture was obviously retouched: Sorge's anxiety was
burdened with someone else's curtained body. One could see the
sharp cut at the verge of his collar, where his head, guillotined
in a shadowy laboratory, was attached to a headless trenchcoat—
plus an inexplicable excess of neck-flesh on the left side.[3] But I
believed that Sorge was in that trenchcoat. I believed that he
was about to enter the door-appari-
tion behind his back. I believed in
the totality of that picture, I believed in the apparent, and I
trusted books. I was ten.

champagne and lobster, with particles of
undigested food thawing on the soles of
their shoes. Some of them were proud
of German air-industry and reliability,
some of them were happy to be alive.

[3] In the early sixties, in the de-Stalinized Soviet Union, the campaign of
Sorge's glorification was set on course and a number of books that contained
Sorge's pictures and previously unrevealed documents from Soviet archives
were published. Most of the books were embellished (if not embroidered)
with, so to speak, fictitious additions. At the same time, a street in Moscow
and a tanker were named after Sorge. In the spring of 1965, the Soviet authorities issued a postage stamp, at the value of 4 kopecks, in his honor. The
commemorative stamp showed Sorge full face on a scarlet background together with a reproduction of the medal of the Hero of the Soviet Union.

In the winter of 1975, I began to conceive the idea that my father[4] was a spy. He had been pursuing a degree at the Leningrad Energy Institute and had often been away, going to Leningrad or Moscow[5] or Siberia or wherever far away. At the 1975 New Year's Eve my father was in the middle of a blizzard, immobilized at the Moscow airport; my mother[6] was staring through the window, watching snowflakes parachuting on Sarajevo; and I was pa-

----

[4] Father: Wilhelm Richard Sorge, a German engineer, a stout man with a nipple-like wart on the nape of his neck and cloudy eyebrows. Working on the Azerbaijan oil fields, when he fell in passionate love with Sorge's mother. Sorge was conceived and born in Baku.

[5] Sorge went to Moscow (from Tokyo, via New York, ostensibly visiting Wiesbaden), for the last time, in 1935. In New York, he encountered, for the last time, Mary Kinzie. In her memoirs, entitled *The History of Nothingness*, Ms. Kinzie depicts Sorge: "When I saw him in 1935 he had become a violent man, a volcanic drinker. Little was left of the charm of the romantic idealist, of the cosmopolitan writer whom I had fallen for on Junker's flight. Nevertheless, he was still extraordinarily good-looking: his cold blue eyes, surrounded by circular darkness, had retained his capacity for vicious self-mockery. He said: 'My personality is split between a man who hates himself and a man whom I hate.' His hair was still potently black, but his cheekbones and sullen mouth were tired" (p. 101).

In Moscow, Sorge visited Yekaterina Maximovna, whom he was believed to have married in 1933, and who died in Siberia in 1943, in a women's camp, her throat cut by a sharp piece of ice in the hand of a jealous working-unit leader. Sorge was looking forward to meeting General Berzin, but General Berzin was gone and was replaced by General Semyon Petrovich Uritsky, who was arrested and shot as a Japanese spy in November of 1937.

trolling our home, vaguely missing my father, anxious to accost Grandpa Frosty (in Socialist Yugoslavia, Santa Claus became Grandpa Frosty and used to arrive on New Year's Eve) at the very moment of his arrival and force him to exchange a plain fountain pen and fluffy sweater (both of which he had sent in advance) for some spy devices. A poisonous fountain pen;[7] a disguise kit[8] (with

[6] Mother: Nina Kobelev, a conventional Russian beauty (big eyes, bony pink cheeks, rotund nose, small mouth with thick lips, cobwebby mustache-shadow, long silky hair, etc.), the daughter of Wilhelm's landlord in Baku. Sorge was born on October 4, 1895, after 37 hours of hard labor. Let us note an obvious thing: Germany was his Fatherland, Russia was his Motherland.

[7] Having agreed to write the full confession, Sorge demanded a (black-and-green) Pelikan fountain pen and a hard-covered notebook with blank sheets. Yoshikawa himself delivered the writing devices. Sorge thanked him and said, in poor Japanese: "Honourable Procurator, this fountain pen is a poisonous fountain pen." Yoshikawa replied: "Honourable Spy, it is the redeeming fountain pen." Then they both laughed.

[8] Sorge never disguised himself, but changed names often. He bragged to Max Klausen that he had more names than women ("And that is a lot, Max!"). He was known as I. K. Sorge, R. Sonter (Moscow 1924–1928); Johann, Sebastian (Sweden, 1928); Christopher, Christian (England, 1929); Johnson, Jim, Gimon, Marlowe (Shanghai, 1930–1932); Richard Sorge (Tokyo, 1933–1944); and there were many other, unknown, evanescent names.

a fake mustache and contact lenses that could change the color of my eyes); a matchbox containing a micro-camera; and a cyanide ampoule, were on the list of my desires. Tired of patrolling and longing, I asked my mother what she would think if I became a spy and she said she wouldn't mind too much, but she would be afraid for me, just as she was afraid for my father and said she would be lonely and sad if I'd change my identity and forget about her and she said she wanted me to be better than my father, not to be somewhere else all the time. That night, falling asleep by the plastic tree, on guard for Grandpa Frosty, I was imagining my father being somewhere else, in a black trench-coat, stealthily walking down a dark hall, stopping in front of a door, looking down the tunnel-like hall behind him, unlocking the door with *something* in his hand, entering the room (my dreamy gaze passing, like a camera, through the wall, following him), finding the desk drawer in the darkness, turning on the desk lamp, turning it away from the window, breaking the lock of the top drawer, taking the matchbox out of his pocket, taking the file out, photographing the documents[9] (with blurred

---

[9] Sorge's activities were much less adventurous than an avid reader would hope. In his written confession, Max Klausen, referring to the years 1933–1939, says: "Six dangerous years passed uneventfully," pointing toward the routine of everyday spying. Sorge's spying meant patiently collecting diverse, and sometimes ostensibly trite, information: a gossip about the Anti-Comintern Pact negotiations; a rumor about the Cabinet changes; the essence of a drunken soldier's swaggering about the military life in Manchuko; someone else's husband being with someone else's wife—useful information for the future Index; air of insurgent desires of young army officers, brought from afar by Miyagi; chitchat among foreign journalists; a careless remark of the German ambassador about "everybody being crazy in Berlin about the Russia attack." In 1936, how-

headings) with the matchbox (whose snapping I attempted to reproduce: "sllt sllt"). But wait, I hear footsteps, heavy thumping, I turn off the light, the footsteps open the door, cut the darkness with the flashlight, like a sword. I'm afraid that he (she?) could smell my fear, my heart is as loud as a tank engine, the door is closed and everything is fine, but I do not dare to be relieved. I uncurtain myself and continue photographing and then I hear a woman sobbing and there is another door and I open the door and a torrent of light rushes in, and a Japanese

----

ever, Sorge obtained a position as the unofficial secretary to the German military attaché, Colonel Ott ("an honest, pleasant, gullible man, with oily military hair, and a thousand and one WWI stories"), and in 1939 he became the German embassy press attaché. This position enabled him to access documents that were considered confidential, even top-secret. Only occasionally he would photograph the document, as in the case of the preliminary document for the Anti-Comintern Pact. Mostly, there was no need for surreptitiousness for he would take any desired document to his improvised office (ex-coffee-kitchen, still reeking of beer from the party celebrating the anniversary of the Hitler ascension) where he would photograph it, or even make notes, at his will. In his article in *Literaturnaya Gazeta* (January 20, 1965), entitled "The Man Who Never Knew Enough," Victor Venykov aptly notes: "A spy is above all a man of politics, who must be able to grasp, analyze and connect in his mind events which seemingly have no connection. He must have the breadth of a historian, the meticulous powers of observation, the spirit and the mind of Tolstoy. Espionage is a continuous and demanding labor and the spy forms himself in that process. Least of all was Sorge like those secret agents whom certain Western authors have created. He did not force open gates in order to steal documents: the documents were shown to him by their very owners. He did not fire his pistol to penetrate the places which he had to penetrate: the doors were graciously opened to him by the guardians of the secret. He did not have to kill. But he was murdered by the brutal machinery."

woman[10] says, with a sorrowful smile: "You must go to bed now. Go undress yourself."

From his journeys to the Soviet Union, my father would bring me dull Soviet toys which all had a sour, oily smell: gray toy car (Volga) that was sticky when touched and produced a hideous high-pitch whining sound when (seldom) driven; dun plastic train station, meant for my long abandoned train; military olive-green gun that ejected little (vomit-orange) plastic balls, in-

----

[10] In October 1935, Sorge met, at the *Rheingold*, Miyake Hinako, a geisha with mild socialist inclinations ("Like many other women I used to read left-wing novels"). She didn't mind Sorge's relentless promiscuity ("It is only natural, isn't it, for a famous man to have several mistresses"). After Sorge's execution, Hanako-san patiently pestered the strict prison authorities to allow her to recover Sorge's body. The ascetic coffin was retrieved from the part of the Sugamo prison cemetery that was reserved for nameless vagrants. Decomposition was rather advanced, and only a large skeleton remained. The large skull (she kissed his ex-forehead) and the bones were those of a foreigner; and there were clear marks of damage to the bones—the eternal result of Sorge's war wounds. Hanako recognized the teeth (and imagined a smile) from their gold filling (from which, in 1946, she had a ring made). She had the coffin removed to the quiet Tama graveyard, just outside Tokyo. "The Society for the Relief of Those Sacrificed in the Ozaki Case" raised funds for Sorge's gravestone, upon which the inscription, in English and Japanese, reads: "Here sleeps the brave stranger who devoted his life to opposing war, and to the struggle for the piece [sic!] of the world." In the early summer of 1965, Hanako-san was invited to visit the Soviet Union. At the Black Sea ("This sea is not as black as our sea"—a polite chuckle from the escorting throng followed) resort of Yalta, Hanako-san saw a performance of *Press Attaché in Tokyo*, a play dealing with Sorge's life in Tokyo, in which she was rendered by a certain Yekaterina Maximovna.

stantly banned and then consequently disposed of by my mother; plethora of books about the victorious Red Army,[11] which I couldn't read since they were in Russian, but I liked the

----

[11] Sorge worked for the Fourth Bureau of the Red Army Intelligence, which none of the members of his ring (Klausen, Voukelitch, Ozaki, Miyagi) knew—they all referred to "the Moscow center" and were happy to work for peace in the world. Jan Karlovich Berzin (real name: Peter Kyuzis) was the all-seeing head of the Fourth Bureau. He was the son of poor Latvian parents, born in Ogre, 1890. At the age of nineteen he was arrested by the Tsarist police for involvement in an assassination plot (a plan to throw a hand grenade at the chief of the Okhrana in the Bolshoi had failed), was sentenced to death and then pardoned because of his youth. He spent some time in prison but surfaced again in 1917 as a member of the Petrograd Bolshevik Party and charged at the Winter Palace. He was the Deputy Minister of Internal Affairs in Soviet Latvia in the spring of 1919, when the military success of the White armies led him to take over command of the Latvian Rifle Division. His first act of command was shooting the previous commander (name lost) with his Luger, having accused, tried, and sentenced him for "revolutionary feebleness" in front of the petrified Rifle Division, right through his left eye (the unfortunate previous commander's brain spurting on the numb political commissar, who later committed suicide). The legend of this execution followed Berzin when he was being made head of the Fourth Bureau and reached Sorge the day before he was to meet him. Berzin and Sorge quickly became friends (Sorge: "I respected his blood-red facial scars and his bright gray hair"). They used nicknames when addressing each other: Berzin was Starik, Sorge was Ika. In 1935, Berzin was arrested and strangled with piano wire (a rather creative execution) as a German spy. It seems that Sorge never found out about Berzin's political death. He never mentioned him, however, after his last visit to Moscow in 1935. Sorge never admitted working for the Red Army, and the Soviet Union maintained, after his arrest, that he had worked for the Comintern, which was supposedly beyond the jurisdiction of the Soviet authorities.

pictures (plain peasant faces, scared stiff of the Army photographer's camera) of the heroes who neutralized a German machine gun by throwing themselves at the barrel or jumped into a terrified German trench, with a cluster of hand grenades attached to their chests. But at the beginning of 1975, after a few cold nights at the airport, he brought me something beyond words: a portable telegraphic system. It was in a gray (naturally) box with a thin booklet, which had a smiling black-and-white boy with gigantic earphones on his head (but no earphones in the box). My father unpacked it: two buzzer-keys and a coil of shining copper wire. Then he put one key in our dining room and the other one in the bedroom (buzz-buzzbuzz-buzz) and the electric current (he said) carrying a Morse-encoded message[12] went over the bedroom floor, passed my father's curled socks (he'd take off his socks first thing when he got back home),

----

[12] The encoded message carrying reports on Sorge's (and his co-spies') activities were sent regularly, although at different, previously agreed upon, times. Max Klausen was the telegraphist (and only the telegraphist). Sorge trusted his blunt ignorance and his ("almost admirable") lack of will. The radio operated from Voukelitch's home in the Bunka apartment complex, across from a rather malodorous canal, named Ochanomizu—"honourable tea-water"; or from Klausen's apartment, in the Akasaka district, with the windows perennially behind curtains of drying bed sheets and underwear; or, almost never, from Sorge's place (No. 30 Nagasaka-cho) in Azabu, an affluent part of the city. The book used for coding messages was an edition of the *Complete Shakespeare*, probably one of the Cambridge editions from the late twenties. Max Klausen: "We would send the number of the play in the book (we called it *the Book*), then the number of the act, then the number of the scene upon which the scramble-code would be based. I had never read Shakespeare and found it quite boring, but Sorge was able to quote

went through the kitchen, speedily crawling by my mother's feet (going to the bathroom to vomit again), then diving under the carpet (lest someone, most likely, I, stumble over and fall onto the glass-top table to be "cut in pieces") of the dining room and then reached the key (buzz-buzzbuzz-buzz) in front of the amazed me. I could not decode the message, so I could not reply, which made me eager to learn Morse code. My father knew Morse code very well (which fueled my suspicions) so he decided to train me. He'd tap messages at the dinner table (my mother digging a crater in the mashed potatoes and rolling her eyes) and I'd try to decode them, forgetting to chew and swallow, the mashed potatoes becoming liquid in my mouth. He'd tap "hurry up" at the bathroom door, where I was getting carried away over a book. I was getting better, I even sent him a couple of simple messages ("want dog"), but my father sus-

----

lengthy passages from any play. I remember once we used a passage, I forgot from which play, where there was a phrase 'God's spies.' Sorge recited the whole passage (I also remember butterflies in that passage) and then said: 'We're God's spies, except there's no God,' and we got a kick out of that and laughed like mad."

(The passage that Klausen alludes to is from *The History of King Lear* and goes as follows:

". . . so we'll live,
And pray, and sing, and tell old tales, and laugh
At gilded butterflies, and hear poor rogues
Talk of court news, and we'll talk with them too—
Who loses and who wins, who's in, who's out,
And take upon's the mystery of things
As if we were God's spies.")

tained his teaching patience only for a week or two, then he was busy, then he was off to the Soviet Union again. I continued practicing Morse code for a while, but then I abandoned practicing because it was boring to send messages into a void. Several times I played a whole spy game: I'd sneak into my parents' bedroom (my mother innocuously watching *The Sound of Music*), photograph the stuff in the top drawer, the unlocked one, of my father's desk (mainly bills) with a matchbox (a *real* matchbox), then I would crawl out of the bedroom, behind the back of my unsuspecting dozing mother, and go to my secret shelter under the glass-top table, and send haplessly coded messages back to the bedroom, imagining that they meant something, picturing someone at the other end of the copper wire. It was all over when I shattered the glass top, almost beheading myself while practicing seeing (seeing clearly, I should say) in the dark—a skill necessary, I believed, for any spy, let alone a great one. My mother terminated the telegraph line and I was left to send messages by telepathy (a brief and only partly successful attempt). When my father came back from the Soviet Union in April, he brought me a too-light, atrociously deformed, pigskin soccer ball.

When my mother went to the hospital to give birth to my little sister Hanna (July 4, 1975–January 31, 1985), my father was away, again. This time he was in Baku, the Soviet Republic of Azerbaijan (whence, in August, he brought me four tin oil-drill towers and a box of little pipes that would have formed a pipeline, had they ever been connected). I was left home alone for lengthy periods of time and was watched over constantly, I believed, by Comrade Tito himself. It was because Branko

Vukelic had told me that one shouldn't use Tito's name in vain, for Comrade Tito had TV monitors at his palace in Belgrade, at which he could see every single resident of Yugoslavia, at any given moment of their lives.[13] "Now," Branko Vukelic said, "if you use Tito's name to swear and then you lie, or if you use

----

[13] On the outset of Sorge's mission to Japan, Berzin told him: "The only thing you should trust and rely upon is the omnipresence of surveillance. There'll be eyes everywhere, and nowhere." Sorge was all too well aware of being watched: even on the Junker flight, he felt a gaze adhered to his body (although that may have been Mary Kinzie). Once in Japan, the following things made Sorge aware of the surveillance:

a) he was being watched by Maritomi Mitsukado, a reporter for *Juji Shimpo,* who would always somehow find him in any bar or at any party and then ask a transparent question like: "Do you think this tyranny will last forever?" (Sorge: "What tyranny?");

b) his maid and laundryman were frequently questioned and tortured by police;

c) a woman he slept with (name lost) got up in the middle of the night and went through his pockets, finding nothing;

d) in bars and restaurants, even at the Imperial Hotel, he was constantly monitored by plainclothesmen of the Thought Police (sticking out of the careless crowd by being too focused on him);

e) his house was searched and his suitcase examined, during his absences;

f) most of all, it was a sense that he developed, a sense that someone's gaze was always at the nape of his neck, like a wart.

Sorge: "When you know you're being watched, you assume a role and play it, even when you sleep—even when you dream. Most of my life I played Richard Sorge, and I was someone else, somewhere else. The ubiquitous surveillance makes everything look differently—you see things through someone else's eyes. Everything is more present—more real—because you see nothing alone."

Tito's name to curse, he can see you. And if he sees you, he may
decide to die and punish us all." I was very careful thereafter not
to swear, lest I be guilty of Comrade Tito's (or someone else's,
for that matter) death. It was soothing to know, however, that I
was being monitored, when I was all by myself, that if someone
came to abduct me (the police or the devil himself) it would
have been seen and I would have been doubtless retrieved from
the sneaky villains. It also meant that I had to wash my hands
after using the bathroom, couldn't pick my nose and stick the

snot to the underside of the chair, nor could I belch like a hog. I
tried to locate the cameras that must have been transmitting images from our home to Tito's residence. While Mother and Father were away, I looked into vases; I looked behind the pictures
on the wall, breaking the one with them in Vienna, on their
honeymoon (for which I was ruthlessly beaten when my mother
came back from the hospital); I looked into lamps and light

switches; I looked everywhere and the only place I could figure
out as a camera location was the TV set (model Futura). It was
a perfectly logical location, for, from the position of the TV, almost every nook of our home was visible—in fact, everything in
the apartment except Mother and Father's bedroom. When I
wanted to be alone, I'd go to their bedroom and lie in their bed,
smelling the ethereal residues of their absent bodies, watching
their wedding picture on the opposite wall (they're smiling,
with a circular lamp behind them acting the moon), still sus-
pecting that there was Tito's camera behind their happiness.

At the time of my poor sister's birth, I was still obsessively
entertaining the idea that my father was a spy, but I hadn't been
able to find any tangible evidence. My suspicions had swollen
because of my father's long phone conferences in Russian with
somebody who had never been identified; because of the letters
(in colorful envelopes embellished with eventful stamps) coming from Moscow, Vladivostok,[14] Stockholm, New York; because
of his mysterious smiles, when he would be watching the news,
as if he knew more than the bland announcers; because of his
comments about the politicians: "He won't last long," or "He's
dead all right"; because of his secluding himself behind the
bedroom door and never letting anyone see what he was doing
there.

When Tito went to Cuba (a TV image of Tito and Castro
hugging, smiles stowed with false teeth: Tito in his white, elaborate field-marshal uniform, Castro in his olive-gray sergeant's
uniform plus the immortal curly beard) I reckoned that I wasn't

---

[14] Sorge's group maintained radio contact mainly with Vladivostok (code
name: "Wittenberg") and, seldom, Moscow (code name: "Munich").

going to be watched or, even if I was, it would be done by some
of his lower officials who wouldn't dwell over me as caringly as
Tito himself would. Thus I decided to venture into going
through my father's drawers, closets, suits, and suitcases, all conveniently located in the bedroom, out of the reach of Tito's men.
I even unplugged the already turned-off TV and put a thick
(Turkmenistan) blanket over it. I took down, carefully, the wedding picture and rolled down the shades. First I went through
(two) suitcases, finding (two) hotel brochures: the Lux[15] in
Moscow and a Holiday Inn in Vienna, with pictures of reception
desks, desolate rooms, and swimming pools. The Lux Hotel
brochure had a smiling Russian beauty (silky braids, rose cheeks,
big eyes, etc.) on the front page. The Holiday Inn brochure had
a picture of a spacious hall, with an immense lantern, dissolved
into glittering crystal tears, hanging from the top of the picture.
I went through the inside suitcase pockets, finding business cards
(in various languages, in sundry alphabets); finding unintelligi-

---

[15] In 1924, upon a decoy invitation from the Moscow Marx-Engels Research
Institute, left by the illustrious scholar Chichikov, Sorge left Germany for
good and went to Moscow. Having spent some weeks in different (apart
from German roaches) apartments, Sorge finally settled in the Lux Hotel,
Room 101. The Lux was the place where all foreign comrades working for
the Comintern lived. Indeed, a day after he took off his socks, poured down
his throat a gigantic glass (with misty fingerprints all over) of vodka and
unpacked his two suitcases (one of which was full of books: *Das Kapital,
Doctor Faustus, Seven Sweet Little Girls,* etc.), he was visited by comrades
Pyatnitski, Kuusinen, Klopstock. The three Comintern activists were infamous for never leaving the proximity of each other ("They were called the
'Three Kings,' but then Klopstock disappeared in the late thirties, I think").
They talked to him all night long, becoming friends along the way, and ef-
fortlessly recruited him for the Comintern Intelligence Division.

ble notes on napkins and exhausted railway tickets; finding a lighter (a miniature camera? No!) and a pack of Soviet cigarettes (Sputnik, with an ostentatious picture of an ascending spaceship on the box); finding mysterious rubber objects (condoms, I was to find out, a couple of years later).

Now I want the reader to assume the role of the camera, to move the objective toward me and peek over my shoulder, following my gaze. I want the camera to focus on the objects that I am about to uncover. I want the thrill of discovery to be ren-

---

PYATNITSKI: "The Comintern is not a party but a world organization of national Communist parties. It toils for world Communism, for the incorporation of the whole world into a single Communist society."

KUUSINEN: "That is, it seeks to do away with private ownership of the means of production, with class exploitation and oppression, with racial tyranny, and to unite nations in accordance with a single master plan."

KLOPSTOCK: "In form and theory, the Comintern is the brains directing activities of the sections as they endeavor to achieve a goal for this stage in the development of world Communism."

ALL: "Welcome!"

In the thirties the Lux Hotel became a virtual detention camp, for foreign comrades were more liable to become foreign spies. The hotel tenants' revolutionary activities were palsied, as they were perennially waiting for the NKVD footsteps to stop before their doors. A car stopping noisily in the middle of the night, in front of the hotel, would have a suicide or two as a consequence. No tenant would let the cleaning personnel into his or her apartment, and after a while cleaning was abandoned altogether. Hence already uncontrollable roaches multiplied exponentially. By 1941, none of the residents from the thirties were left in the hotel, apart from now gigantic cockroaches and a comrade from Yugoslavia, mad and dying, preserved only due to a careless bureaucratic error.

dered with the exactness of the detail. I want this to be docu-
mented. Turn on the light. Roll.

The left closet. First the underwear. You have to look under
the neatly built pyramid of undershirts. Nothing. Under the
panties. A book, with pictures: *Figurae Veneris—A Love
Manual.*[16] Men and women, naked, assuming acrobatic positions, hairy crotches. Never mind. Towels. Nothing. Bedspreads.
A cloth-covered notebook, with Mother's name written on it,
with a lock, no key. Hell. Leave it as if nothing happened. Now
the drawer. Sheets of paper, documents, sorted into three sepa-

---

[16] Beside *German Imperialism* (1927), a study of the political will that led
to the slaughter of WWI, and *The Accumulation of Capital and Rosa Luxemburg* (1922), a study of the life and theories of the great German revolutionary, Sorge's most important work was *Marxism and Love* (1921), a
work about human relationships in the context of merciless exploitation. In
the Introduction, Sorge writes: "Thus love is not possible in a class society,
for every human relationship is a relationship of property, exploitation, and
ideological subjugation. Love as a concept can be achieved only in a class-
less society, where a man is a man and a woman is a woman. Just as the de-
cisive intensification of class struggle, exposing the cruelty of capitalism,
leads towards the revolution, the intensification of purely sexual relations
would expose the inhumanity of individual human relations. The conse-
quent objectified vacuum of inhumanity would simply require a revolutionary action. Love, to sum up, is not what we need now—what we need
now is sex!" Scholars claim that *Marxism and Love* is more a product of the
unfulfilled desire for Christiane, the wife of Kurt Gerlach, his teacher at
the Kiel University, than a product of studious research. Some, however,
tried to show that *Marxism and Love* (and some articles like "Anal Sex and
Revolution" from 1923) influenced Wilhelm Reich. Sorge himself was not
too proud of his early theoretical work: "I am convinced that my handling
of these difficult theoretical questions was cumbersome and immature, and
I hope that the Nazis burned every last copy."

rate, puzzling, stacks. First stack: floor plans of a house,[17] plus charts with numbers summoned at the bottom of the last page: 1,782, twice underlined. Second stack: diplomas and resumes. Flip through: "... worked to develop more efficient ways of transmitting energy ... particularly interested in international nets ... Sincerely." Third stack: four files. First file: receipts. Second file: paid bills. Third file: a diploma: "... is hereby confirmed to have graduated at the University of Sarajevo and to have attained the title of *Engineer and Energy Transmission Manager*." Fourth file: pictures from the wedding. Mother

---

[17] Sorge's house was what the Japanese in those days called a *bunka jutaku*, or "an up-to-date residence," which was, by contemporary European and American standards, rather small. Alphonse Kauders, who visited Sorge in 1939, described it as "scarcely more than a two-story doghouse in a small garden." In the upstairs room that Sorge used as his study, the untidiness that surrounded him amused his friends (Kauders: "It was like a Verdun of things") and horrified his housemaid ("German pig!"), for there was a seeming chaos of books, maps, magazines, and papers. Kauders recalls that many of the books were on economics (notably on the geisha wage system), that there were American movie magazines (obtained from Gimon), and that there was "some quite interesting Asian pornography." There were one or two fine Japanese prints and some expensive pieces of bronze and china. There were photographs of Japanese creek dams and a photograph of Greta Garbo on the thin walls. The room also contained a gramophone, and a pet owl (fed with local mice and cockroaches) in a cage. Sorge respected Japanese customs by removing his shoes at the front door and by wearing velvet slippers on the stairs and in the tiny corridor. He slept in Japanese fashion, on a mattress laid on the *tatami*, with his head on a small round, hard pillow. Kauders, describing Sorge's bathroom, remembers that the fanatically clean Sorge "scrubbed himself daily, as if there was no tomorrow, and then, drawing up his knees, climbed into the wooden tub, filled with scorchingly hot water."

holding the wedding wreath. Father touching her above the left elbow, as if pushing her to step across the edges of the picture. Mother laughing, with her chin up. Father is about to spread his arms in a gesture of asking. Mother and Father in the center of the picture, a man and a woman stepping into the picture from opposite sides, with symmetrical grins. Father hugging the woman whose back is turned toward the camera (zoom). A twinkle of sweat on Father's forehead. Mother hugging the woman (zoom). Tears reaching the nostrils. On each picture a globe lamp behind them: dazzling, fake, immobile moon. Cut.

The middle closet. Roll. First, the shelf above the suits. Boxes of slides, almost all of them from the USSR, the rest from vacations on the Adriatic coast. Random picks: the cracked Tsar's Knoll and my father minute by its side; Father between two guards in front of the Lenin Mausoleum: Father sending a smile toward the camera, the two identical guards behind his back, eternally erecting their left legs, with skillfully expressionless faces and the slender rifles pointing toward the respective upper corners of the picture. Mother, Father in

bathing suits and myself in a baby suit in the front, and Grandpa[18] and Grandma behind us (Grandma wearing a

[18] Sorge's grandfather, Adolph Sorge, had served as the secretary for the First International during Marx's lifetime. Grandpa Adolph told Sorge, throughout his childhood, Marx stories: about Marx reading Shakespeare (in English)

black scarf and a buttoned-up black dress), on a pebbly beach, with three towels, like welcome rugs, at our feet. Look at this: Father's camera (Laika) and a cylindrical plastic box containing a telescopic lens. A bottle of Valium[19] ("Keep out of reach of children"). A stack of blank sheets. A box of envelopes. An address book. A: Aliluyev, Alexander, rue de Victorie 101, Paris; B: Bulgakov, Sergei, Andreyevski Uzhvis 45, Kiev; V: Vadimovich, Vladimir, P. O. Box 6165, Geneva. A glass, with the Sputnik (leaving the diminishing planet behind) painted on it, full of pens and unsharpened, virgin pencils. A black-and-green Pelikan fountain pen. A heap of hotel brochures: the Luxembourg Hotel, Paris—a smiling chef over a stove, with unidentifiable blots ostensibly sizzling in the pan; the Tripoli

----

and the Greek tragedies (in Greek) every July; about Marx and Engels playing tennis (Marx always losing), as the officials of the First International watched them, moving their heads "left-right, left-right, like a clock pendulum"; about Grandpa Adolph, stopping by Marx's home and taking him to a bogus meeting, covering Marx's secret trysts with his (recently fired) housemaid; about Marx's pathological fear of dentists—Engels or Grandpa having to go with him and hold his hand as the blood soaked his immortal beard; about holding, piously, the manuscript of *The Communist Manifesto*, knowing that it was something that was to change the world forever, "the world that philosophers theretofore only attempted to interpret."

[19] During his stay in Shanghai, Sorge was a frequent visitor of the infamous opium houses. In 1932, in the middle of the siege of Shanghai, in Gong Li's opium bar, Sorge had a sensation of the physically split personality: Sorge stepped out of his own body and left it to wallow in its opiatic stupor, while he walked among the defenders, with a German nostalgia for trenches, handing out grenades to poorly clad and armed Chinese, not fearing Japanese bullets, hallucinating about "the eye of the ubiquitous sniper, the infinite preciseness of the supreme sharpshooter."

Hotel, Tripoli—a hall with dismal sofas summoned around a forlorn table, as vacuous as if every form of life was terminated by the flashbulb. A pocket notebook (zoom) with pairs of English and Serbo-Croatian words: birth—*rodjenje;* blind— *slijep;* work—*rad;* arrest—*hapsiti;* son—*sin;* mother—*majka;* money—*novac;* death—*smrt.* The right closet. Let's go through his suits. Blue suit: nothing. Blue suit two: nothing. Black suit: nothing in outer pockets, a personal thermometer in the inside pocket. Gray suit: the Party[20] membership card, a key, a piece of paper, with a local phone number (zoom) with an "S" above it, a pack of matches (Aeroflot), a plastic spoon, a red-white-blue marble. White suit: nothing in the outer pockets, nothing in the inside pockets. Except the little pocket down here. It's a tiny plastic cylinder, like a bottle of pills, with a gray lid, you have to press the lid down, there's a film inside (could I have more light, please), unrolling: snapshots (nega-

---

[20] Sorge was admitted to the Tokyo branch of the Nazi Party in October 1934. In his speech, preceding an orgiastic drinking contest, Colonel Ott said: "One cannot but feel that our cause will be only strengthened by the energy of Dr. Richard Sorge, our beloved fellow German. There's no better occasion to use, once again, our Führer's timeless words: 'We have hundred of thousands of the most intelligent sons of peasants and workers. We will have them educated and are already doing so, and we wish them someday to occupy the leading positions of state and society, along the rest of our educated strata, and not the members of the alien people. We are determined to thwart and thrust aside this alien people that knew how to insinuate itself and seize all the leading positions for itself, for we want our own people for that position.' I deeply believe that Dr. Richard Sorge's blood will only enhance the purity of German blood. Welcome, Richard, welcome!"

tives) of papers, one after the other, thirty-four of them, last two shots are of a river dam, it seems, and there is a miniature figure (zoom, damn it), no—can't see. What's on the papers? They look like documents (headings blurred), they seem to be in Russian. Would you turn off that camera and leave the room please; I need some privacy, I have just obtained proof that my father is a spy.[21]

Besides greasy toys (for me) and large cans of pickled fish (for my mother) my father brought stories from the USSR: about his travels down the Volga River, passing by towns, one after the other, made of cubicles, factory smokestacks, and an enormous Lenin statue (making a step forward, pointing toward the future); about the greatest dam in the world, on the Yenisey

----

[21] The Thought Police inspectors, with the typical bureaucratic thoroughness, made an inventory of the items seized at Sorge's house upon the arrest. Those bare objects—the physical tools of espionage—were to form the first grim and material skeleton in the body of proof to be forged against him. They included three cameras; one copying camera with accessories; three photo lenses (one telescopic); developing equipment; two rolls of film with photographed documents (the nature of the documents is unknown from the police files); one black leather wallet containing $1,782; sixteen notebooks with details of contacts with agents and notes in an unknown language; Sorge's Nazi Party card (with membership fees paid until 1951) and a list of Party members in Japan; two volumes of the *Complete Shakespeare* (no data as to what edition); seven pages of reports and charts in English; and, lastly and fatally, two pages of a typewritten draft, also in English, of the final message of achievement, compiled to be sent to "Wittenberg" on October 15.

River—watching the boiling river at the foot of the dam was "like watching the Red Sea splitting"; about the Turkmenistan people who rode purebred horses as if they'd grown out of them; about thousands of miles of taiga, where prehistoric creatures lived and where you'd never be found if you were lost; about places so cold that your blood would just stop flowing if you stopped moving; about places where vodka was so cheap that

nobody drank water. Many stories featured Professor Venykov— my father always referred to him as Professor Venykov, as if that was his christened name. The stories of Venykov were stories of placidity: about long conversations by the always warm samovar, with affordable caviar and pickled pike liver; about walks down the Nevski Prospekt, while Russian children played hockey on the frozen Neva; about Venykov reminiscing about his childhood: cherry orchards around Kiev, swimming in the Dnieper, fighting, at the age of nineteen, as a partisan in the last war;[22] about his beautiful wife and two girls who were solving complicated mathematical problems when not playing piano-cello duets; about chess games[23] in the community sauna. My father claimed that Venykov's home was his home in the Soviet Union.

In the late summer of 1976, upon a fabricated invitation from the Sarajevo Micronet Research Institute (which my father obtained through his connections), Professor Venykov

----

[22] Sorge: "In the summer of 1914, I visited Sweden on vacation, and returned to Germany by the last boat available. The Austrian Archduke had been assassinated in Sarajevo, and World War I broke out. I volunteered for service immediately, joining the army without reporting to my school or taking the final graduation examination." This period may be described as "from the schoolhouse to the slaughterhouse." Sorge was sent to the Eastern Front (Galicia). He was befriended by an old stonesman from Hamburg, a real leftist, whose head was shattered to smithereens before Sorge's very eyes, a piece of skull bone cutting his face (a permanent scar remained). In July 1915, Sorge was wounded by shrapnel in his right leg. In 1916, a bullet struck him from the back, taking out his bowels. Sorge was transported to a field hospital, conscious, watching with listless amazement his viscera throbbing in his hands. Exhausted surgeons gave him no hope of survival, but patched him up and let him occupy a bed. Sorge's next-bed neighbor, a Jewish boy, crushed his skull against the bed frame, as Sorge was helplessly writhing in his own pain. In early 1917, fully and miraculously recovered, Sorge was sent back to the Galician front, where he became one of the best sharpshooters in his division, specializing in eliminating enemy snipers.

[23] Sorge was a passionate chess player. He played against Kurt Gerlach (Sorge: 25—Gerlach: 50); Pyatnitski, Kuusinen, Klopstock (Sorge: 12—Pyatnitski, Kuusinen, Klopstock: 12); Berzin (Sorge: 131—Berzin: 127); Klausen (Sorge: 1—Klausen: 0); Ozaki (Sorge: 50—Ozaki: 49); Hanako (Sorge: 111—Hanako: 0); Ott (Sorge: 45—Ott: 12); and he played against himself daily.

came to visit us. He arrived at five o'clock in the morning, having driven nonstop for sixteen hours, from Budapest to Sarajevo (only a sip of vodka, once in a while, to keep him awake). He avoided ringing the bell and cautiously knocked at our door, not quite being there. Father and Mother hesitantly left the bed (Mother taking Hanna in her arms), exchanging timorous glances, not being able to step out of their respective dreams. My father looked through the peephole ("Professor Venykov!"), opened the door and snatched him inside, looking down the hall before closing the door. They exchanged exclamations for a while (Father: "Professor Venykov!" Venykov: *"Ay, moy Pyotr! Moy Pyotr!"*) then my father pointed toward my mother and me, making a motion with his hands as if opening the door behind which we were hidden *("Molodyets, Pyotr! Molodyets!")*. Venykov had a pear-shaped body on the top of which there was a bald head (with a wart, like a miniature knob, on his forehead). His eyes were tired—red cracks were rushing toward turquoise irises. Behind the smell-screen of sweat, onion, and vodka, I could still discern the oily odor of my toys.

Venykov had a bath and shaved, but wore the same shirt as before (a white shirt with a pear-pattern, including leaves on the stalks). We had breakfast—Venykov enthusiastically ate away a heap of bananas (Mother informing me, by a weighty glance, that bananas are not to be touched, except by Venykov), entirely ignoring the boiled eggs and sausage. "It's hard to come across bananas in Leningrad," my father translated Venykov's banana-peeling remark. After the breakfast, Venykov opened one of his (two) suitcases and pulled out, one by one, a throng of rotund *matyoshky* (we already had dozens on a remote shelf). Then he put a bottle (Stolichnaya), wrapped in a sheet of *Literaturnaya Gazeta*, in my father's hands. As my father was peeling the bottle, Venykov was dismantling *matyoshky*, echoing each other, all facing different directions, as if blind. *"Nuh!"* Venykov said, touching the head of the largest *matyoshka*. *"Nuh!"*

That night we all watched *Brigadoon* on TV (Venykov mumbling, *"Duraky!"*) Despite my father's protests, he went

to sleep in his car—a Volga resembling a gigantic black cockroach, parked in front of our apartment building.

"Why doesn't he sleep here?" I asked.

"He feels uncomfortable in a foreign country," Father said. "He's afraid of being treated as someone other than himself."

I had been more or less convinced that my father was a spy, and I somehow learned to live with it. I could still catch a shadow passing over his face—a shadow of something that he had been doing and nobody was supposed to know about. He was still making phone calls in Russian, and the film multiplied. Venykov delivered to him an envelope, and he locked it in the lower drawer of his desk. The conversations they had in Russian, behind the bedroom door, or walking ahead of my mother and me, never sounded like conversations—rather like lectures or briefings. I couldn't, however, make myself believe that Venykov was a spy—not once I saw him peeling a banana (his gaze following the descent of the peel) or devouring a baklava, or humming with Julie Andrews and making his hand dance in rhythm, while watching *The Sound of Music.* I figured that he could be a benign cover or just a naïve courier.[24]

The Venykov weeks passed uneventfully: he was playing chess with my father (Mother: "What's the score?" Father: "One thirty-one—one twenty-seven."); visiting the mountains around Sarajevo; buying cheap Italian jeans from smugglers for his girls (a smuggler to his accomplice: "Get me size thirty

----

[24] Sorge: "Legitimate and plausible cover is absolutely essential for a spy. I worked as a news reporter and found that the foreign correspondent is conveniently situated for the acquisition of information of various types, but that he's closely observed by the police. I believe, however, that the best thing an agent can do is render himself an intellectual: a professor, a writer, a scholar. Generally speaking, the intellectual class is made up of men of average or less than average intelligence, and the agent who assumes such a cover would be quite safe from detection by police. Moreover, as an intellectual with extensive scholarly connections (which he would utilize as sources or transmitters of information) he could associate with people who possess information they know nothing about, he could ask ostensibly ludicrous questions and develop trust. I think that intellectuals are the pets of the world, digging holes in the backyards of history. They can move around without arousing suspicion."

for Brezhnev!"); going to movies[25] *(You Only Live Twice, From Russia with Love, True Stories VI);* talking to my father behind the closed doors. We'd watch his Volga, before going to sleep, seeing flashes of flesh as he was putting on his crimson pajamas. Near the end of the third week, at the end of the day that included a movie *(Arabian Nights),* a dinner (Bosnian cuisine),

---

[25] In the files of the Frankfurt Police, dating from 1927, there is a vague and unconfirmed report showing that a Dr. Richard Sorge left for the United States on January 24, 1926, and spent some time in California, working in Hollywood film studios. The only admission, however, made by Sorge of visiting America was on his way to Japan. Herr Alexander Hemon, a researcher at the German Foreign Office Archives, claims that there is a possibility that Dr. Richard Sorge, identified by the police as being in Frankfurt in 1925 and 1926, was "not the Soviet spy who was working in Tokyo and on mysterious missions abroad, but someone else, of whom we know nothing."

and plenty of delectable Turkish coffee, Venykov agreed to sleep in my room. Lying between my parents (my sister in her crib), I could hear the hum of Venykov's snoring, occasionally interrupted by the smacking of his lips. Mother: "He's not going to stay forever, is he?" Father: "He's got to go back. His wife and children are there." Me: "Why can't they come here?" Father: "They just can't."

The following day, Venykov packed up before any of us got up (although my sister bawled pitilessly, alarming us, I suppose), had a quick breakfast with us, then kissed my forehead, shook his index finger with my sister, hugged my mother and father (slapping his back dramatically), turned on the cockroach-car, and drove back to Leningrad. "He's home," announced my father two days later, after a brief phone conversation. In my room, Venykov left the scent of his newly purchased aftershave (Pitralon) and a crumpled brown sock under my bed.

In October 1977, my father was arrested.[26] There were no screeching cars in the middle of the night, no marble-faced men in leather coats, no terrified, shivering neighbors too

----

[26] On the evening of Tuesday, October 7th, 1941, Sorge had arranged a customary meeting with Ozaki at the Asia Restaurant, in the South Manchurian Railway building. He kept the appointment in vain, devouring sake, absentmindedly flirting with a woman ("a Mary Kinzie look-alike"), gorging on *escargot* at the next table. Miyagi was due to come to Sorge's house two days later, but failed to appear. On Friday, October 10th, Klausen and Voukelitch called on Sorge, by a prior arrangement, in an atmosphere of mounting disquiet. Voukelitch telephoned Ozaki's office and

scared to look through the peephole, no breaking doors—not even loud fist-banging at the door. They simply called him on the phone. He hung up and said to my mother: "They want me about some traffic violation. It must be a misunderstanding. I'll be back shortly." He put tennis shoes (Puma) on his bare feet and was gone. He did not come back home that sleepless night or the day after. My mother was tirelessly making frantic phone calls, none of which lasted more than one or two minutes, for nobody wanted to talk to her. Her dread was increasing, and she was trying to repress it (soundlessly sobbing), while Hanna moaned all the time (refusing to eat her liquid foods). My entertaining the idea that Father was a spy had never been much more than a way to embellish my vacant childhood, but with Father's arrest, it suddenly became palpable. My spine tingled with the pride in the ability to sense his spyness, while, at the same

---

received no answer. Klausen: "The air was heavy, and Sorge said gravely— as if our fate was sealed—'Neither Joe nor Otto showed up to meet us. They must have been arrested by the police.' "

After Voukelitch and Klausen left Sorge's house and strayed toward their respective fates (Voukelitch: died of typhus in the prison hospital; Klausen: scorched in his prison cell by an American bomb during an air raid), Sorge could not rest and instead made frantic love to Hanako, who was gentler and smoother than ever. At two o'clock after midnight, a plainclothesman (name lost), with two uniformed, sleepy policemen, knocked politely on Sorge's door and, receiving no answer (Sorge and Hanako approaching another climax), shouted: "We have come to see you about your recent traffic accident." Sorge appeared at the door in pajamas and slippers and then was, without further exchange, bundled into an inconspicuously black police car, protesting (in whisper, so as not to wake his neighbors) that his arrest was illegal.

time, I was scared, beginning to realize that we were up against something beyond my feeble comprehension. My limbs became weightier and larger, my motion beyond my control. I constantly felt an urge to hide under the bed or in the closet, but all I could do was watch my mother swing (with ululating Hanna in her arms) back and forth, like a metronome.

Four days after my father's vanishing, Slobodan came. He rang the bell patiently, while my mother was alternately looking through the peephole and at me, deliberating whether to open the door. "I'm a friend," Slobodan announced. My mother opened the door, but kept it chained. "Madam," he said and showed her the inside of his wallet. "I'm Inspector[27] Slobodan." "State security," my mother mumbled. "No need to behave like a hysterical woman," he said. "I'm here to help." Mother unchained the door and let him in. He went straight to the dining room, without taking his shoes off, sat down and

---

[27] The procurator directly responsible for the interrogation of Sorge was Yoshikawa Mitsusada of the Thought Department of the Tokyo District Court Procurator Bureau. Yoshikawa had an extensive knowledge of current political and economic thought, including Marxism. It was rumored that he had been a Marxist himself when he was a student at Tokyo Imperial University. Soon after graduating from the university, he had written a comprehensive study of the geisha wage system. It seems that there was some mutual admiration between the two of them. Yoshikawa: "In my whole life, I have never seen anyone as great as he was." After the sentence, at their last meeting, Sorge asked Yoshikawa to be kind to Hanako-san: "She will marry a professor in the end and have a boring and happy life. Don't do anything to her."

wiped his thick glasses and vast forehead with a handkerchief, while Mother and I watched him benumbed.

"I want you to know, madam, that we know everything.[28] We have watched, we have listened, we know," he said. "And I also want you to know that we have no hard feelings about you. We presume that you knew nothing of your husband's activities. Had you known, you would have informed us, am I right? Feel free to interrupt me. I just feel that that pretty mouth of

---

[28] Some of Sorge's information, seemingly petty, was passed on by way of the Fourth Bureau to the GPU, which used it to build the foundations for what would become the KGB's Sixth Division of the First Directorate— the infamous Index. The Index was a vast collection of biographical and personal data about everyone who might, even very remotely, be of use at some time or another, to Soviet espionage. The Index files contained information about sexual preferences (obtained by voyeuristic monitoring or tempting agents); eating (restaurant bills, etc.), and sleeping (calls in the middle of the night, monitoring, etc.) habits; about sports teams affiliations; about reading interests (subscription lists, library records, etc.) and, often, recorded stories, apparently unrelated, which helped the one in charge of the particular individual to assess what sort of person he or she was to utilize. The information could be used for blackmail, or for assuming the right approach when recruiting, or for plugging damaging information into the public's mind. Cold War defectors brought numerous stories about the Index and, almost without exception, claimed that the official slogan was "We know everything!" In pre-computer times, only the Nazi Gestapo had much the same kind of organization, but it was not nearly as detailed nor all embracing as the Index. There are claims, dating all the way from the sixties, that the United States Government agencies (CIA, FBI, or both) are building a computer database, based on the principles similar to the Index's, but none of those claims has ever been confirmed.

yours wants to start clattering. Cute children, madam. Are they yours? Just joking—they look *exactly* like you. What's the little girl's name? She'll be an attractive woman, I'll tell you. Feel free to interrupt me. You shouldn't feel that way about me, madam. I'm a nice person. I love this country, you know, I think that we have something here, something like no other place in the world and I can tell you that there are plenty of people who think that way. We don't want this country, what our fathers bled for, to be defiled—it belongs to us and we want to keep it. And if you don't like it—well, you're welcome to leave and go somewhere else, to America[29] or wherever the hell you want. Don't you agree with me? Tell me, don't you think the same way?"

My mother said: "Comrade Slobodan, I want you to leave this very moment!"

"I'll be glad to do so, but not before I take care of several wee things. I need a nice photograph of your husband, for the papers. No? Well, I'll take the liberty of looking for this and

----

[29] Major General Charles A. Willoughby, MacArthur's Chief of Intelligence (1941–1951), confiscated all the Japanese Sorge files that survived the leveling of Tokyo and conducted an investigation of the Sorge case, which helped uncover many a Communist network back home in the United States of America. In his book *Shanghai Conspiracy: The Sorge Spy Ring* (1952) he aptly notes: "Though the work of Dr. Richard Sorge and his companions belongs to history, the methods of their work should serve as a clear warning for today and for the future. They concern not just the intelligence officer but every good citizen. Some of the implications are frightening. One begins to wonder whom one can trust, what innocent-appearing friend may suddenly be discovered as an enemy."

that. You may watch—lest I be tempted to take something for myself."

My mother retched several times, then put Hanna into the crib and hurried to the bathroom. I heard her vomiting, as if coughing.

"Women, always vomiting. Stay away from women, little boy, that's my advice. So, tell me about your father. Do you like your daddy? I suppose you do. When I was a boy, I always had a place where I would hide precious little things, you know, marbles, and ticklish pictures and stuff. Do you have a place like that? Does your father have a place like that? Would you show me?

My mother walked back in.

"I was just asking your boy, madam, what does he want to be in his life: What do you want to be, young man?"

"A journalist," I said.

"Smart, very smart. You're going to get very far, my boy. Madam, if you'd show me where your husband keeps his private stuff, I'd be thankful beyond words. No? Well, then I'll just look around, if you don't mind."

He got up and paced around the dining room, pulled out a couple of books from the shelf, flipped through them detachedly, and put them back. He turned toward us, smiled, said: "Pardon me," and slipped into the bedroom.

Mother and I heard noises coming from the bedroom: thumping of suitcases, a screech of a drawer, a snap of a locked drawer, din of sundry things being thrown on the floor. Mother held my hand, squeezing it—her hand, moist and faint. Slobodan walked out with a suitcase, shoving something into his pocket. He produced a little box (with a painted bee landing on a flower) out of his hand and said: "Condoms, my boy. Had your father had this on, you would have rotted, stuck in a sewage pipe, years ago." My mother plucked the box out of his hand and said: "Get out!"

"If you wish to talk to me, feel free to call me. My boss always says that love has political limits.[30] Please, call me." He wrote the phone number on the wall by the front door: 71–782, then opened the door and walked out. Before my mother closed the door, he shouted in the echoing hall: "We should get together sometime, now that you're alone."

Mother reluctantly opened the bedroom door: an open suitcase; a pile of suits (hanger-hooks looking like bowed swan heads); the Sputnik glass shattered, pens and pencils scattered around, like corpses. On the bed, there were two symmetrical foot-shaped dents, and mounted ripples on the bedspread around them.

After a month or so, Hanna and I went with our mother to

[30] In August 1941, Hanako-san was summoned to the Thought Police headquarters and urged by a man named Nakamura to break off relations with Sorge ("They don't know what loyalty means! They don't know the value of the family!"). The typically Sorgean, sardonic reaction was to invite Nakamura to dinner—an invitation that was embarrassingly ignored.

visit Father in jail. The visiting room looked like a decrepit hotel hall, with stained and torn sofas and armchairs sorted into separate throngs. Father came followed by a guard[31] in a wan blue uniform (the rim of his cap touching the top of his eyebrows). Mother immediately burst into tears and hugged Father. He sat down between Hanna ("Tata! Tata!") and me, putting his arms around us (thin, bloody wristlets). The tip of his left eyetooth was broken and under his left ear, at the root of the jaw, there was a huge bruise, as if a shadow of the ear.

"I've done nothing wrong," he said.

"Shut your fucking mouth!" roared the guard.

"Did they torture[32] you?" Mother asked.

"A slap or two."

"Shut your fucking mouth!"

---

[31] In the Sugamo prison, Sorge was befriended, somewhat surprisingly, by Captain Ohashi—the head of the guards. After Sorge had written his confession, Ohashi brought newspapers to Sugamo everyday, together with a supply of Sorge's own tea. Sometimes, they'd drink tea together in Sorge's cell (Sorge: "If I am sentenced to death, Captain Ohashi, I shall become a ghost and haunt you"). In October 1944, after the execution day had been set, Ohashi bought some fruit and sake and gave what he described as a "farewell party" for Sorge. Ohashi begged a farewell gift from Sorge— preferably Sorge's black Italian shoes with leather soles and silk laces. After Sorge was led to the execution, the polished pair of shoes was found in his cell (toes facing the wall), with folded silk socks inside, and a note for Ohashi: "I will never forget your kindness during the most difficult time of my eventful life."

[32] Before getting to Yoshikawa, Sorge went through the obligatory interrogation conducted by lower procurators, which chiefly meant rather routine torture: Sorge was compelled to remain in a kneeling position, in formal

"How's your school?" Father asked me.

"Fine."

"He got the best grade in the class[33] on the history test."

"Good," he said. "Good."

"What do they want from you?" Mother asked.

"They're interrogating me. They want me to sign a statement."[34]

"Shut your big fucking mouth! This is the last time I'm telling you."

Father was sentenced, after a brief (closed to the public)

Japanese style, for hours, while three procurators struck him repeatedly, stamped their feet on his knees, or twisted his head and arms in a judo hold. On occasions, they'd burn hair or pierced particularly painful points (nipples, testicles, anus) on his body. Every once in a while Sorge would just close his eyes and try to ignore the immense pain. The momentary trance would be smashed by a full-fist blow from behind to his ear or the nape of his neck—the pain would be so intense that Sorge vomited uncontrollably. Naturally, he did not sign the confession under torture.

[33] While in high school, Sorge's best friend was a Jewish boy named Franz, with whom he shared an interest in German history—particularly Barbarossa and Bismarck. The friendship was abruptly broken off after Franz tried to kiss Ika, over the book about Barbarossa's incursion, full of pictures of heavily armored German knights on stout curtained horses.

[34] Sorge broke down in the Buddhist chaplain's room in Sugamo, after the signed statements by Klausen, Voukelitch, Ozaki, and Miyagi were shown to him. Yoshikawa made the following appeal: "What about your obligations as a human being? Your friends, who have risked their lives and families to work with you, for *your* cause, have confessed and may hope thereby to secure some mitigation, however slight, of their sentences. Are you going to abandon them to their fate? Are you going to betray them? Are you going to

trial, to three years of hard labor and was shipped off to the Zenica prison on January 7, 1978. There was footage shown on TV of my father (and four obscure men) in the courtroom hand-cuffed, as the voice-over spoke about "disseminating foreign pro-paganda," about "the internal enemy who never sleeps," about "Tito and his vision," about "protecting what our fathers bled for."

"We have seen it before," the voice said. "And we'll see it again: dissembling intellectuals, spreading dissent like a lethal germ. But this is what we have to tell them: stay away from the clear stream of our progress or we'll crush you like snails!"[35]

The years of Father's imprisonment passed uneventfully: my sister was growing, learning to speak, learning to be sad; my mother became reticent; and I was going through all those adolescent things: the deepening of the voice, rebelling, read-ing *(The Stranger, The Trial, The Metamorphosis)*; falling in

----

be remembered as a typical Western man, caring more about himself than anyone else? If I were in your place, I'd confess." Sorge said: "Honourable Procurator, I have been defeated, for which I congratulate you," after which he requested the pen (black-and-green Pelikan) and paper (blank sheet, hard-cover notebook). He wrote an autobiographical confession, which amounted to some 50,000 words and began with the words: "For the first time in my life, I want to tell the truth: I have been a Communist since 1928."

[35] Neither the German, Japanese, nor Soviet public was ever informed about Sorge's trial and execution. Indeed, there was no official acknowledgment from any of the governments, apart from a brief cable from the German am-bassador (recently promoted ex-Colonel Ott) in Tokyo, closing the case as far as Berlin was concerned: "The German journalist Richard Sorge who, as previously reported, has been condemned to death for espionage on behalf of

love (a Nina, until her father forbade her seeing me). But I participated in all this half-heartedly, as if it were all happening to someone else and I was watching it with languid amazement. No one was visiting us and we were going nowhere. Only Slobodan would call once in a while ("Your father is locked behind walls with desperate men, my boy, and your mother needs all the support she can get"). Once a month, we'd go to see Father. We'd sit on the bench in the prison yard, even in the winter, exchanging petty information about our walled-off lives, too aware of the gaze of the remote guards and the sharpshooter in the watchtower. In the spring of 1979, Mother and Father sat on the bench, for two hours, mainly mute, while I was catching stray butterflies for Hanna, and morose prisoners, staring at each other's napes, revolved around a guard (chanting: "Left-right! Left-right!"). When we came back home (after a two-hour ride in a bus full of drunken, vomiting soldiers) Mother burst into tears while unbuttoning her (black) shirt, sat on the chair and wept for hours, ignoring my repeated questions, pushing me away.

In September 1979, I wrote my first poem,[36] in less than an hour, as if hallucinating. The poem was entitled "The Loneliest Man in the World." It was about Sorge and it was more vicarious self-pitying than anything else. I'm translating it (in fact, only the

---

the Soviet Union, was, according to a communication from the Foreign Ministry, hanged on November 7th." (Let us note a well-known fact: November 7, 1944, was the twenty-seventh anniversary of the October Revolution.)

[36] In 1919, Sorge wrote a poem which began with the line: "Eternally a stranger, fleeing from himself " and read it in the Gerlach's salon before the

first of ten tedious stanzas) from memory, for I annihilated the
notebook (with other, much less memorable, poems) at the peak
of the campaign of self-loathing and destruction[37] (which also included shaving every single hair on my body) in my late teens:

Tokyo is breathing and I am not,
The curtain of rain glued to my face.
I don't live a life, I live a plot,
Having two selves in one place etc.

----

audience of leftist university professors, Christiane, and Kurt himself. Kurt
Gerlach mercilessly mocked Sorge's poetic instincts: "'Fleeing from himself'—bah! Where would you go? That's bourgeois gibberish, Ika. Man is a
product of social relations—formed in history by history—not a self, not
an essence hoarded in the center of the metaphysical fluff. 'Eternally a
stranger'—bah!" Sorge burned the sheet with his poem and made no literary attempts (his confession notwithstanding) for the rest of his life.

[37] After the disastrous courting attempt, driven by the choking desire for
Christiane ("Dear Ika! I have liked you, even your self-mocking and sardonic wit. But what you did last night is not what a decent woman can
bear . . ."), Sorge attempted suicide. Lacking courage to end his life with
his mind clear, he fueled his death wishes with cheap pear schnapps,
while a razor lay, ominously, on the table before him. The courage, however, reached its zenith after the second glass, declining rapidly thereafter, until he passed out. He woke up sixteen hours later (reeking of
vomit, emptied of schnapps) not knowing where he was or why he was
there. After that unfortunate incident, he would see Christiane only from
afar, embers of his former desire suffocating under the ashes of orgiastic
rampages.

I wanted to show it to my father, next time we went to visit him, but he was ill and he only wanted to know about the Afghanistan events[38] (political prisoners could not watch the news). This time we met him in a miasmic room, with a small window looking at the women's prison. He was escorted by a guard, whom he nicknamed "Barabas," and who would help him get up or walk ("You can put me back on the cross now, Barabas"). The prison uniform was dangling from his now scrawny shoulders. "I shrank," he said.

In January 1980, Father was released from prison, diagnosed with brain cancer, curled into an old man, with most of his teeth missing. He could wear my clothes, and the wedding ring was sliding down his finger—he took it off. We rearranged our place and put the TV in the bedroom, Father taking hold of the remote for the rest of his life. He'd watch TV (mainly the news) all day, sucking a banana, occasionally passing out and then waking up from listless

----

[38] During Sorge's preliminary trial, Stalingrad was under siege. Sorge, who perceived that this was the battlefield where the war was to be decided, took great interest in news about the battle. He'd ask Yoshikawa in the court, whispering, about Stalingrad, while the judge would be talking to his clerk. Yoshikawa would reply in undertone, telling him about the general situation ("They're keeping their positions," or "It looks good"). The preliminary judge knew what was going on, but did nothing to stop them. When Stalingrad was saved, Ohashi watched Sorge, through the peephole of his cell, dancing, clapping hands, and kissing the walls with joy.

dreams. On his good days, he'd be drinking strong-scented tea[39] and tell us stories about his USSR journeys: about Ukrainian weddings, everybody dancing *kolomiyka* like there was no tomorrow; about nuclear submarines that could stay for days under water (crews going blind); about riding camels in Kazakhstan; about wheat fields spreading as far as you could see and beyond. Every day, he was getting smaller and smaller, as if flesh was being squeezed out of him like toothpaste.

On May 4, Comrade Tito died. He had been ailing for a long time and they had had to amputate his leg. We were, for days, repeatedly shown footage of (monopedic) Comrade Tito smiling, surrounded by glowing doctors (happier than anyone that he was alive), a wrinkleless sheet covering his retained leg. Sirens began wailing at 15:04. I looked through the window and saw everything still: people stood motionless on the street, cars were paralyzed, as if someone had stopped the film in the projector. On the black TV screen white letters emitted: "Comrade Tito has passed away"—no voice-over, no images shown. Sirens stopped wailing. I looked at the street and everybody and everything was gone, as if the

---

[39] Moments before the execution, the chief chaplain of the Sugamo prison (accompanied by Yoshikawa and Ohashi) offered Sorge tea and cake and said: "Life and death are one and the same thing to one who has attained personal beatitude. Impersonal beatitude can be attained by entrusting everything to the mercy of Buddha." Sorge said: "I thank you, but: no!"

ground had gaped open and swallowed it all.[40] "I suppose this is Judgment Day," my father said and turned off the TV. "I suppose this is the end of it all."

---

[40] Sorge was led into a vaporous, windowless, bare room, with a gallows standing in the center. He was led across the room and placed beneath the gallows, while a noose was affixed around his neck. There was no staircase to climb, no platform to stand on. The trap was in the floor, immediately beneath his feet.

THE ACCORDION

1

The horses are trotting stolidly and the coach is bobbing steadily, and Archduke Franz Ferdinand's eyelids are listlessly sliding down his corneas. The weighty eyelids are about to reach the bottom, but then the horse on the left raises its tail—embarrassingly similar to the tussock on the Archduke's resplendent helmet—and the Archduke can see the horse's anus slowly opening, like a camera aperture.

The coach is passing between two tentacles of an ostensibly exultant throng: they wave little flags and cheer in some monkey language ("Would it be called Bosnian?" wonders the Archduke). Children with filthy faces and putrid, cracked teeth run up and down between the legs of the crowd. The Archduke recognizes the secret police, with their impeccable mustaches, with stern, black hats that look clearly grotesque among blood-red fezzes—much like topsy-turvy flower pots with short tassels—and women with little curtains over their faces. The secret police stand stiff, throwing skillful side glances, waiting for the opportunity to show off their alertness. The left horse is dropping turds, like dark, deflated tennis balls. The shallow, obscure river behind the back of the Archduke's foreign, cunning denizens is reeking of rotten sauerkraut. In the coach ahead, the Archduke can see only the top of General Potiorek's ceremonial helmet: the elaborate tussock is fluttering annoyingly. He decides to get rid of Potiorek as soon as he assumes the throne.

The Archduke looks at the Archduchess and sees her face in a cramp of disgust. "It would be very unseemly if she started vomiting again in front of all these people," he thinks. He touches her (cool) hand, carefully trying to convey his manly concern, but she turns to him with the unchanged sickened face and the Archduke quickly recoils.

The coach rolls between two cordons of smirking people waving ridiculous, tiny flags, and vapid, marble-faced secret policemen. The Archduke then sees a man with an accordion stretched over his chest. The man is smiling, sincerely, it appears—he may even be delighted. He doesn't seem to be playing the accordion, just holding it. The Archduke's gaze breaks through the crowd and he can now see the man's strong arms and the accordion belts squeezing the man's strong forearms. He can see the beige-and-black keyboard and he can see that one of the keys is missing; he can see the dark rectangle in place of the missing key. The coach passes the man and the Archduke thinks he can sense the man's gaze on his back. He's tempted to turn around, but that would obviously be unseemly. The Archduke wonders about these strange people, about this man who doesn't seem to possess any hatred toward him and the Empire (not yet, at least) and he begins to wonder what happened to that key. Can you play a song without that key? How would *Liebestod* sound with one of the notes never being played? Maybe that man never played that key; maybe he'll never play that note in his entire life. "Strange people," thinks the Archduke. He decides to tell the Archduchess about the man with the accordion, perhaps it could cheer her up.

"There's a man with an accordion," announces the Archduke into the Archduchess's ear. The Archduchess winces, as though he's delirious.

"What? What are you talking about?"

He leans toward her: "There's a man . . ."

But then he sees a pistol and a straight, tense arm behind

it and a young, scrawny man at the end of the arm, with a thin mustache and fiery eyes. He sees the pistol retching and bursts of light at the pistol's mouth. He feels something pushing him against the seat and then it punches him in his belly and all the sounds have disappeared.

Besides the quick-swelling, incomprehensible fear that he can do nothing about and tries to ignore, all he can think of is an evening at Mayerling: the Archduchess played *Liebestod* on the piano, much too slowly, while he sat in the armchair by the fireplace, feeling the heat on the left side of his back. He wasn't listening to the Archduchess, he was struggling not to doze off, and then he had a rapid thought—which he immediately suppressed—oh my God, how vernacular and ungraceful was the Archduchess's beauty and how unbearably vapid and stupid *Liebestod* really was.

He wants to tell her he's painfully sorry, now, but the Archduchess, her face frozen in repulsion, the Archduchess is already dead.

2

Most of this story is a consequence of irresponsible imagination and shameless speculation. (A case in point: the Archduke died in a car, which took a wrong turn and then virtually parked in front of the assassin, whose pants were soaked with urine.) Parts of it, however, washed against my shores, having floated on a sea of history books, dotted with islands of black-and-white photographs. A considerable part reached me after it passed through tunnels and mazes of the family memories and legends. For the man with the accordion was none other than my great-grandfather, freshly arrived in Bosnia from

Ukraine. He was in Sarajevo, for the first and only time in his life, to obtain papers for the promised piece of land—the bait that brought him to Bosnia—from the Austro-Hungarian Empire. He was a peasant and had never been in a big city. The fuss and giddiness that he encountered in the city blessed by the Archduke's visit (and then cursed by his death) overwhelmed him, so much so that he spent nearly a fifth of his savings to buy the accordion from a Gypsy at the city market. By the time he got back to his new home, on a hill called Vucijak, the First World War was well on its way. He was recruited within a couple of weeks and went to Galicia to fight for the Empire, where he died of dysentery. The accordion outlived him by some fifty cacophonic years, losing a few more keys along the way. It met its demise with a discordant accordion sigh, after my blind uncle Teodor (a hand grenade had exploded in his hands when he was six) threw himself on the bed where the accordion helplessly lay. Uncle Teodor is now stuck in the Serb part of Bosnia. Most of my family is scattered across Canada. This story was written in Chicago (where I live) on the subway, after a long day of arduous work as a parking assistant, A.D. 1996.

EXCHANGE

OF

PLEASANT WORDS

1

What year was it? We have chosen to believe it was 1811. Therefore: In the fall of 1811, Alexandre Hemon got up from his slothful bed in Quimper, Brittany; sold, unbeknownst to his widowed mother, their only horse—a perennially exhausted nag—for thirty silver coins; and joined, after some adventurous drifting, Napoleon's army on its way to Russia, heading for yet another glorious victory. He was, we believe, twenty-one at the time. We imagine him marching through Prussia, still stunned by the greatness of the world; crossing the Nieman river in June 1812, the river washing down a gossamer coat of dust and cooling off his sore, blistering feet. Then we can see him charging at the ferocious Russians at Smolensk. At Borodino, he leads the infantry attack armed with a sabre; he single-handedly captures a battery of begging-for-mercy Russians. ("No, Lev, that was not a victory!" my father might exclaim when narrating this particular stretch of the family history.) We watch with him the flames of Moscow scalding the sky's belly. But there's no joy any longer in his extinguished heart: the victories don't seem to be so wholesome anymore, and his sore feet have changed state—now they're frozen solid. Then comes the humiliating, murderous retreat. The officers are nowhere in sight, the soldier next to you just soundlessly drops in the snow like an icicle, then never gets up, and the Russians keep mauling the mutilated body of the great army. He stumbles and falls through the snow-laden steppe and when he raises his head he's in the midst of a thick forest.

We know very well that the route of Napoleon's army's

retreat went through what is today Belorussia and there's no plausible explanation for Alexandre ending up in the western Ukraine, near Lvov. Certain factions in the family suggested that higher forces had had a hand in the miraculous (mis)placement of Alexandre. My father—who deems himself to be the foremost authority on the family history and one of its main narrators—dismisses the implausibility with a derisive frown, providing as evidence a map of Ukraine, dating from 1932, on which Smolensk (for example) is just inches away from Lvov.

Be that as it may, Alexandre went astray from the straight road of defeat and found himself, unconscious, in the midst of a pitch-dark forest. He had drifted to the edge of the eternal black hole, when someone pulled him out of it, tugging his benumbed leg. There's hardly any doubt that that was the great-great-grandmother Marija. Alexandre opened his eyes and saw the angelic smile of a seventeen-year-old girl trying to take off his decrepit, yet still precious, boots. Let me confess that a blasphemous thought has occurred to me: the angelic smile might have been missing a considerable number of teeth, due to the then-common winter scurvy. She, naturally, decided to take him home, unloading the firewood and mounting him on the tired nag (somehow, that was the epoch of tired nags). Her parents, surprised and scared, could not resist her determination, so she made him a bed near the hearth and then nursed him out of his glacial numbness, patiently rubbing his limbs to get the blood started. (Uncle Teodor sometimes likes to add a touch of gangrene at this point.) She fed him honey and lard, and spoke to him mellifluously. Yes, she rekindled his heart and they did get married. Yes, they're considered to be the Adam and Eve of the Hemon universe.

My mother, who proudly descends from a sturdy stock of

Bosnian peasantry, considered all this to be the typical "Hemon propaganda." And she may well have been right, I'm afraid to say. For we have no well-established facts from which the unquestionable existence of Alexandre Hemon would necessarily follow. There is, however, some circumstantial evidence:

a) At the time of the Winter Olympics in Sarajevo, my sister held in her hand a credit card in the name of a certain Lucien Hemon. Lucien was the rifle manager for the French biathlon team. He told my sister, not hesitating to flirt with her, that Hemon was a rather common family name in Brittany and suggested, after she had managed to tell him the highlights of the family history, that a Napoleonic soldier could have well carried it over to Ukraine. That was the germ from which Alexandre sprung, and the previously dominant theory that "Hemon" was a Ukrainian variation on "demon" was indefinitely suspended.

b) In 1990, a busload of excited Bosnian Ukrainians went to Ukraine in order to perform a set of old songs and dances, long forgotten in the oppressed ex-homeland. While they were staying in a waterless hotel in Lvov, the Hemons decided to venture into the village (Ostaloveschy) that my great-grandfather's family had left to move to Bosnia. I should point out that there was a widespread belief in the family that we had no kin in Ukraine. As they snooped around the depressed village, mainly populated by bored-to-senility elderly folks, they aroused plenty of suspicion among the villagers, who must have believed that the KGB was onto them again. In antique Ukrainian, just for the hell of it, they questioned toothless men leaning on their canes and fences about Hemons in the village, until one of them pointed peevishly at the house across the dirt road. The man in the house told them that, yes, he was a

Hemon, but had no knowledge of any kin in Bosnia. He out-
right told them that he was no fool and that he knew they
worked for the police. They tried to dissuade him from throwing them out, pointing out that police agents and spies do not
move around in such large and compact groups—there were
fourteen of them, all vaguely resembling one another and scar-
ing the wits out of their poor distant cousin. Next day, the man
(his name was, not surprisingly, Ivan) visited them in their dismal hotel, considerately bringing a bottle of water as a gift.
They told him, trying to outshout each other, about the exodus
to Bosnia, about the family beekeeping, about the legendary
Alexandre Hemon. Yes, he told them, he might have heard
about a Frenchman being related to the family a long time ago.

Thus it was definitely established by the family that our
tree was rooted in glorious Brittany, which clearly distinguished us from other Ukrainians—a people of priests and
peasants—let alone Bosnian Ukrainians. Once Alexandre
Hemon was officially admitted to the family, the interest for
things Gallic surged (and no one much cared for the nuanced
differences between the Bretons and the French). My father
would unblinkingly and determinedly sit through an entire
French movie—French movies used to bore him out of his
mind—and then would claim some sort of genetic understanding of the intricate relations between characters in, say, *À
Bout de Souffle*. He went so far as to claim that my cousin
Vlado was the spitting image of Jean-Paul Belmondo, which
consequently made Vlado (a handsome blond young man)
begin referring to himself as "Belmondo." "Belmondo is hungry," he would announce to his mother upon returning from
work in a leather factory.

Further developments in the Hemon family-name history
were propelled—I'm proud to say—by my literary exploits. In

the course of attaining my useless comparative literature degree at the University of Sarajevo, I read *The Iliad* and found a lightning reference to "Hemon the Mighty." Then I read *Antigone*, where I discovered that Antigone's suicidal fiancé was named Hemon—Hemon pronounced as Haemon, just like our family name. In the agon with Creon, Hemon at first looks like a suck-up:

> My father, I am yours. You keep me straight
> with your good judgment, which I shall ever follow.
> Nor shall a marriage count for more with me
> than your kind leading.

But then they get into a real argument, and Hemon tells Creon off: "No city is a property of a single man," and "You'd rule a desert beautifully alone," and "If you weren't a father, I should call you mad."

My father dutifully copied the one page from *The Iliad* that, toward the bottom, had "Hemon the Mighty" and the handful of pages in *Antigone* where the unfortunate Hemon agonizes with the cocky Creon. He highlighted every sighting of the Hemon name with a blindingly yellow marker. He kept showing the copies to his co-workers, poor creatures with generic Slavic surnames, which—at best!—might have signified a minor character in a socialist-realist novel, someone, say, whose life is saved by the fearless main character, or who simply and insignificantly dies. My father didn't bother to read *Antigone*, never mind tens of thousands of lines of *The Iliad*, and I failed to mention to him that "Hemon the Mighty" is absolutely irrelevant in the great epic and that Antigone's illustrious fiancé committed not-so-illustrious suicide by hanging himself.

The following semester, I found a Hemon in *The Aeneid*, where he makes a fleeting appearance as a chief of a savage tribe. Sure enough, my father added the promptly highlighted photocopy to his Hemon archive. Finally, in *Gargantua and Pantagruel*, I stumbled upon "Hemon and his four sons" involved in an outrageous Rabelaisan orgy. The Rabelais reference, however, provided the missing link with the French chapter of the family history, which now could be swiftly reconstructed all the way back to 2000 B.C.

There is, unfortunately, a shadow stretching over this respectable history, a trace of murky, Biblical past that no one dared to follow but which the designated, though inept, historian feels obliged to mention: My cousin Aleksandra still remembers the timor and terror she felt when, in church, she heard the priest utter—clearly and loudly—our name. The priest, she says, described a man who stood in the murderous crowd under the cross on which Our Savior was expiring in incomprehensible pain, his eyes (the man's, of course) bulging with evil, bloodthirsty saliva running down his inhuman chin, laughing away Our Savior's suffering. "What kind of man is he?" thundered the priest. "What kind of man could laugh at the Lamb's slaughter? *Hemon* was his name, and we know that his seed was winnowed and scattered all over this doomed earth, eternally miserable, alone and deprived of God's love." Stricken with horror (she was nine), she retched and ran out, while her father, my uncle Roman, who was not paying attention, kept saying "Amen!"

Later investigations found no Hemons in the Bible, although it is entirely unclear who the researcher was and how exactly the research was conducted. The official explanation, accepted by the entire family, was that the priest was performing an act of vicious revenge, probably because my Aunt

Amalija called him "a pig in the vestment" while the wrong ears were listening, or because my father married a communist.

In any case, few thought that we carried the mortifying burden of the ancient sin on our shoulders, or that we would have a family reunion in hell. "We have always been honest, hard-working people," my father announced to the priest who replaced the hostile one (who had moved to Canada), pointing his finger toward the ceiling, beyond which, presumably, there was the supreme judge and avenger. The priest amicably nodded and accepted a bottle of home-made slivovitz and a jar of first-class honey, with which the potentially eternal dispute between the Hemons and God (regarding his Son) was settled, it seemed then, satisfactorily for both parties.

I have had doubts, however, along with some of my younger cousins and a very close relative. I have had doubts and fears that indeed we could have committed the terrible sin of sniggering at someone else's suffering. Perhaps that's why we emigrated, again, in the 1990s, from Bosnia to the United States. Perhaps this is the punishment: we have to live these half-lives of people who cannot forget what they used to be and who are afraid of being addressed in a foreign language, not being able any longer to utter anything truly meaningful. I have seen my parents, mute, in an elevator, in Schaumburg, Illinois, staring at their uncomfortable toes, stowed in foreign shoes, as a breezy English-speaking neighbor entered the elevator and attempted to commence a conversation about the unkind Midwestern weather. My father kept pressing the buttons 11 and 18 (where the verbose American was heading), as if they were supposed to terminate the fucking multilingual world and take us all back to the time before the Tower of Babel was unwisely built and history began to unwind in the wrong, inhuman direction. My mother occasionally grinned painfully at the confounded neighbor, as the elevator rose arduously, through the molasses of silence, to the eleventh floor.

2

Inspired by the success of the Sarajevo Olympiad and the newly established ancient family history, the family council, headed righteously by my father, decided to have an epic get-together, which was to be held only once, and was to be recorded as the Hemoniad. The minutes from that family council meeting (taken by me) can scarcely convey the excitement and joyous awareness of the event's future importance. Allow me to step out of my worn-out historian's shoes and become a witness for an instant: I can attest that there was a moment of comprehensive silence—a fly was heard buzzing stubbornly against the window pane; fire was cracking in the stove; someone's bowels disrespectfully grumbled—a moment when everyone looked into the future marked by the Hemoniad, the event that would make even our Homeric cousins envious. Even Grandfather, in one of his precious lucid moments, seemed to recognize everyone and did not ask "Where am I?" as he normally did. The magic was dispelled when the milk pot boiled over, and a swarm of aunts flew toward the stove to repair the damage.

Thus it was decided that the Hemoniad was to be held in June 1991, at my grandparents' estate, which was falling apart because of my grandfather's dotage, but was, nevertheless, "the place where our roots still hold the land together, fighting cadaverous worms." It was also decided that the Hemons should reach out to the Hemuns, the family branch that grew out of the tree trunk of Uncle Ilyko, my grandfather's brother.

This is their history: Uncle Ilyko went from Bosnia to Ukraine to fight for Ukrainian independence in 1917. After the humiliating defeat, in 1921, he walked to the newly formed border between Romania and Yugoslavia, where they arrested him and put him on the train back to Kiev. He jumped off the train somewhere in Bukovina, and then roamed, as the first snow of the year, ominously abundant, was smothering the earth. He almost froze to death, but was found and saved by a young war widow, who nursed him out of glacial darkness all winter, asking for nothing from him but to warm her cold feet and dilute her loneliness. In the spring, he got up from the shaky bed, took from her trembling hands a bundle with knit socks, a brick of cheese, and a daguerreotype of her. He kissed her tearful cheeks, including a hirsute wart, and walked, only at night, back to the Romanian-Yugoslav border. Sometime in the spring of 1922, he swam across the Danube, whose murky, cold waters dissolved the daguerreotype.

Well, we never liked him. He was a violent, impetuous man. The day Ilyko returned home—where everyone thought he had long been dead—he got into a fight with Grandfather, because my grandfather had married the girl Ilyko had had a crush on. Infuriated, he went to Indjija, Serbia, married a native, and let a drunk clerk change his name to Hemun, which became the original sin of the Hemun branch. Indeed, the Hemuns avoided contact with the descendants of my grandparents, barely spoke Ukrainian, sang no Ukrainian songs, danced no Ukrainian dances, and thought of themselves as Serbs. The Hemuns, then, were to be saved from "the weed of otherness," and come back to the forest of flesh and bone growing out of the ancient Hemon roots. When they told

Grandfather that the Hemuns were to come back to their historic home, he—God bless him—asked: "And who are they?"

In the weeks after the family council meeting, the invitation was forged in the Olympic minds of Uncle Teodor and my father. Uncle Teodor made suggestions, and my father rejected them as he typed. Let me submit an image: Uncle Teodor running different formulations by my father: ". . . the branch that was unjustly severed . . . the branch that fell off and broke the tree's heart . . . the branch that shriveled, detached from its roots . . ." My father's index fingers leaping up and down the typing keyboard, like virgins dancing for gods—Father occasionally using a virgin to pick his nose, and saying: "No . . . no . . . no . . . no . . ." As with all the great documents of history, the Hemoniad invitation went through many drafts and finally attained the form of exceptional grace and power. It clearly stated the purpose (". . . to reattach the most formidable branch to its just place . . ."); the place (". . . the Hemon family estate, where thousands of years of history are told by bees and birds and chickens . . ."); the logistics (". . . we shall feast on spit-roast piglets and mixed salad, and if you need cakes and pastry, you are advised to make them yourselves . . ."); the structure (". . . spare time will be spent in the house, in the courtyard, in the backyard, in the field, in the orchard, in the apiary, in the garden, in the cowshed, by the creek, in the forest, in conversation and exchange of pleasant words . . ."). The invitation was gladly received by many, and responses from all corners of the family began pouring in. The participation of many Hemuns was heralded by a phone call from the oldest Hemun, Andrija, and a tide of elation advanced through the family. Oh, those days when planning a piglet slaughter over the phone had mythological proportions; when old stories were excavated from the basements of memory, and then polished and embellished; when sleepless, warm nights were wasted in trying to make sleeping arrangements, until Uncle Teodor suggested the hay under the cowshed roof, where "the youth" could sleep; when my mother kept rolling her eyes, suspicious of any mass meeting of people of the same ethnicity; when aunts independently met to organize the cake-and-pastry production, lest we have a surfeit of *balabushki.*

I'm afraid this sentence was inescapable: the day of the Hemoniad arrived. A huge tent had been put up, above a long table. The stage for "the orchestra" had been built under the walnut tree in the center of the courtyard. Uncle Teodor, they say, was up at dawn, sitting on the porch and rehearsing the stories for the last time. I woke up (here we have a personal memory) to the incessant warbling of birds nesting under the roof. When I descended the stairs, I saw a pair of dancing headless chickens, trying to run away from something (but couldn't because it was everywhere) their wings arrhythmically flapping, blood spurting out of their necks in decreasing streams. We had breakfast, sitting around the big table, passing panfuls of fried chicken livers and hearts, and platefuls of sliced tomatoes and pickles. "This," said Uncle Teodor, "is the greatest day of my life."

The Hemuns arrived all at once, with a fleet of shining new cars, like a colonizing army. They were uniformly over-weight and spoke with a northern-Serbian drawl, which implied a life of affluent leisure. Nonetheless, everyone hugged each other, cheeks were smacked with kisses, hands were shaken ardently, and backs were slapped to the point of bruising. Uncle Teodor hollered: "Welcome, Hemuns!" and then proceeded from Hemun to Hemun, offering them his stump. He would turn his ear to each of them, asking: "And who are you?" and then memorized their voices.

The day went on in an atmosphere of general merriment and pleasant conversing. We have images, recorded on video, of the crowd in the tent, milling in a perpetual attempt to get closer to each other, like atoms forced to form a molecule, as everyone merged into one big body, with moist armpits and indestructible vocal chords. The band played all day, on and off, led by my cousin Ivan, who kept winking, over his heavily breathing accordion, at every woman under forty not directly related to him. When the band played old Ukrainian songs, the Hemuns sat grinning, confounded and embarrassed, for they could not understand a word. But everyone danced in whatever way they could, waltzing clumsily, their hands adhering to their partner's bobbing sides and sweaty palms; or, their stage-fright temporarily cured by an infusion of a helpful beverage (beer was my choice of the courage-helper), they would dance *kolomiyka*, spinning at different speeds, from neck-breaking to mere circular trotting.

Around one o'clock, as the sun got stuck right above the walnut-tree top, my six aunts ascended the stage, having been introduced by Uncle Teodor, who recited their hypocoristic names like a poem: "Halyka, Malyka, Natalyka, Marenyka, Julyka, Filyka." They sang a song about a young Ukrainian soldier who was being sent off to die in yet another battle for the freedom of Ukraine, who was doing what most of the soldiers in most of the Ukrainian songs did all the time: he was saying good-bye to his inconsolable mother and his faithful bride-to-be. They sang (my aunts) with their arms propped akimbo, serenely swaying and rubbing each other's elbows. They looked like six variations of the same woman. Grandfather suddenly pricked up his ears, as if recognizing the song, but then he was retaken by the demons of slumber and succumbed with a grunt. Meanwhile, the soldier died (as we all had expected) and his faithful bride-to-be was about to be ravished by the same force that was to enslave Ukraine. "This song," explained Uncle Teodor, after my aunts bowed, blushed, and scuttled off the stage, "is about the value of freedom and independence."

Then the lunch was served and everyone sat around the long table, with Grandfather floating on the Lethe at the head of the table. The table was creaking under heaps of pork and chicken limbs. There were big-ear soup bowls, which were reverently passed around the table, as steam was enthusiastically gushing up, like smoke from a snoozy volcano. There were plates of green onions, stacked like timber, and tomato slices sunk in their own slobber. After the lunch, everyone became drowsy, descending from the mountains of meat to the lowlands of sleep. Snippets of conversation died off within instants, for no one's blood was capable of reaching the brain. Grandfather was fast asleep and snoring, leaning on his sagely stick. He burped in his sleep and moved his tongue over his upper lip, touching the bottom of the mustache, and then in the opposite direction along the lower lip, for a whiff of pleasant taste had escaped the inferno of slow digestion and reached his palate. Finally, everything yielded to the stupor, and excited flies could land, after a long journey, on the continent abundant with meat and salad. They would comfortably sit on a slice of bread, greasing themselves to dazzling summer-fly glitter. Abruptly they would ascend, as if to check whether they could still fly. They would go down again, buzzing messages of festive pleasure to each other. Watching them, it occurred to me that they were our flies—Hemon flies—and therefore better than other flies, oblivious to their historical role.

On the videotape of the Hemoniad, the only document of the glorious festivity that reached the United States, this transcendental, cadaverous torpor is contained within three or four intense minutes of silence, the hum of the breeze in the microphone notwithstanding. It is important to note, however, that the flies disappeared in the process of converting the tape from PAL-SECAM to NTSC.

Then Uncle Teodor was snatched out of his wheezing tranquillity and led to the stage, where he was placed into a chair. The level of consciousness abruptly rose around the table. Uncle Teodor said: "I will tell you stories now, because it is important to know one's own history. If you know the stories, just sit quiet and listen—we have people who don't know them." The Hemuns—people who didn't know the stories— fidgeted and glanced timorously at each other, for they suspected that the stories would present them as treacherous and weak people. But Uncle Teodor had different intentions. He began with the Hemons of *The Iliad*, their doughty feats and their contribution to the burning of Troy. Then he talked about the Hemon who almost married Antigone, the most beautiful woman of the ancient world. He barely touched on the Hemon who was Aeneas' sidekick and who founded the Roman empire with him. He talked about Hemons defending the European civilization from a deluge of barbarian Slavic marauders. Then he skipped a number of centuries and nearly brought tears to everyone's eyes talking about the murderous retreat and Alexandre's travails and the horrors of Russian winter. He told us of Alexandre's hallucinations: armies of headless men, marching in circles, and he trying to escape a gigantic ax that strived to decapitate him, until he fell down— "he didn't feel the snap, but he felt blood spurting and the cold slowly gnawing his limbs." And then he was saved by our Ur-Mother Marija. As Uncle Teodor was narrating their budding love and Alexandre's recovery, Grandfather burst to the surface of the day, looked around in genuine astonishment and asked me, since I was sitting next to him:

"Who are these people?"

I said: "They're your tribe, Grandpa."

"I've never seen them in my life."

"Yes, you have, Grandpa."

"And who are you?"

"I'm one of your grandchildren."

"I've never seen you in my life."

"Well, now you can see me."

"Where are we?"

"We're home, Grandpa."

That seemed to satisfy him, so he dropped his head to his chest, and was back in the boat crossing the Lethe. In the meantime, Uncle Teodor got to Alexandre and Marija's progeny. The Hemons of the mid-nineteenth century were invariably bright and dexterous and hard-working, even though they perennially suffered from Polish and Russian injustice, plus tuberculosis and scurvy. Moreover, women kept miscarrying, while men kept falling off trees and being gored by disobedient cattle. "And yet we survived!" exclaimed Uncle Teodor. He went on to tell a story I had never heard before, a story about the ancestor who had gone to America to become a rich man, and when he became a rich man he returned to his village. He built a beautiful house and did nothing but court rural virgins, receive and drink with guests. One of his drinking acquaintances, probably the devil incarnate, dared him to spend a night on the local graveyard, which was known to be haunted by the village Jews massacred in a pogrom. He bet his whole estate that he would spend the night and he did, but he met the rose-fingered dawn with his hair completely white and his hands unstoppably shaking. He never told anyone what he had heard or seen, but the next day he gave all he had to the rabbi of the few remaining Jews so he could build a home for the wandering spirits. He was deemed insane after that by his relatives, who had just gotten used to being members of a wealthy family, and who claimed that it was Jewish magic that cast a spell on their dear cousin. One day he disappeared, and no one ever saw him again. Uncle Teodor claimed that he had gone back to America, and that we probably have some American cousins. As we imagined our half-mad white-haired cousin sailing toward the Statue of Liberty, coffee was served. We sipped strong tarrish liquid from a demitasse, without really noticing that Uncle Teodor had omitted the second half of the nineteenth century (probably because some of our forefathers were prone to pogrom fever) and began telling the narrative about the exodus to Bosnia.

Imagine the crushing poverty, the year-long drought and cattle plague, the bone-cracking cold of the 1914 winter, the widespread banditry of hungry, destitute ex-peasants—we all writhed in our seats, fretting the unforeseeable future with our ancestors. Great-grandparents Teodor and Marija, the story went, packed all they had: a few bundles of poorly patched clothing; a beehive, sealed to make the trip; some clay pots and a coal iron; a roll of money they had saved up, which spent the trip in my great-grandmother's bosom absorbing sweat and entertaining lice. Grandfather, presently dozing off next to me, and Ilyko fought throughout the journey. They had been given a piece of uncultivated land—"this very land"—which was now "the best piece of land in Bosnia," although, to tell the truth, it produced nothing but retarded corn and shriveled apples. Great-grandfather went to Sarajevo to get the papers for the land on the day the Archduke Franz Ferdinand was killed. He bought an accordion there, "this very accordion," which was not true, for Uncle Teodor himself crushed the accordion some years ago. Oh, the years of struggling and working from the sun up to the sun down. And then Ilyko went to fight the Bolsheviks—"We all know what happened then, and that is why we are all here now."

It was the Hemuns who got impatient first, and their impatience quickly became contagious. As Uncle Teodor, entirely carried away, continued talking about Uncle Julius and his twenty-five years in Stalin's camps, both the Hemuns and the Hemons kept rising, hastening towards the outhouse, pouring slivovitz down their throats, chitchatting, anything but listen to the blind narrator. By the time Uncle Julius got to the Arkhangelsk camp, where he was to be sentenced to death, no one—except me—was listening. My father stood up and said: "Enough, Teodor. You'll continue later." But he never did, for the band started playing again and everybody was imbibing elating beverages. Again shoulders were slapped, crushing hugs and smacking kisses generously exchanged, while dancing, even if in slow motion, seemed to be approaching trance. Some of it could be seen on the videotape, but not without effort, because I had one drink too many, and the camera was held by my tremulous hands. Thus the image is shaking and leaping, which, incidentally, works well in showing the ubiquitous giddiness. As the camera was taken away from me, so was my clear-mindedness, and everything became dizzy and dim. Allow me to submit several discontinuous memories—memories of images and sensations that flashed before the helpless mind's eye, as the mind capsized and sank to the sandy bottom of complete oblivion: the noxious, sour manure stench coming from the pigsty; the howling of the only piglet left alive; the fluttering of fleeting chickens; pungent smoke, coming from moribund pig-roast fires; relentless shuffling and rustle of the gravel on which many feet danced; my aunts and other auntly women trodding the *kolomiyka* on the gravel; their ankles universally swollen, and their skin-hued stockings descending slowly down their varicose calves; the scent of a pine plank and the prickly coarseness of its surface, as I laid my cheek on it and everything spun, as if I were in a washing machine; my cousin Ivan's sandaled left foot tap-tap-tapping on the stage, headed by its rotund big toe; the vast fields of cakes and pastries arrayed on the bed (on which my grandmother had expired), meticulously sorted in chocolate and non-chocolate phalanxes; the intense, chewy taste of green onions and pork that washed off my palate, immediately followed by a billow of gastric acid; greasy itchiness around my mouth, adumbrating numerous, putrid pimples; the chained dog, hysterical and aroused, jumping at me, nearly choking himself and coating my hands and face with his drool; the seething warmth of the concrete steps, in the proximity of the dog, where I attempted to regain my seasick consciousness; the needly hay under the revolving roof of the cowshed; my hand holding a long, crooked stick (a Napoleonic sword), beating a nettle throng (Russian soldiers), and my forearms burning and rubicund; truckloads of helmeted soldiers, passing by the house, shooting in the air, and showing us the three-fingered sign, shouting and throwing bottles at chickens; trucks dragging erected cannons, and dark jeeps following them; an unfamiliar cat, caught as it was stealthily jumping on the table strewn with gnawed bones and splinters of meat, staring at me, the pupils stretched to the edges in utter feline disbelief, as if I were not supposed to be there, as if my vomitous existence had not been approved by the being whose approval the cat clearly had.

Then I was sitting down on the grass, leaning against the

walnut tree, then closing my eyes and carefully searching for the position in which my head would stop gyrating. I put the tips of my index fingers against my temples, and thus fixed my head, not daring to blink, let alone to move. I heard the din of voices, the garrulous babel, the uproar of guttural excitement, which all eventually ebbed. Then I could hear (although I'm not sure I did) my father's voice, "wishing to conclude this epic festival of Hemonhood, with words that could not possibly match the greatness of the occasion." He talked about our ancient roots and "thousands of years of Hemonian diligence," which helped us survive the biggest catastrophes in human memory. "Do you think it is an accident that our ancestor Alexandre was one of the few to survive the unfathomable defeat of Napoleon's army? Do you think it is just luck that he progressed through several heart-chilling blizzards to meet the woman of his life, the Eve of the Hemon universe?" No one dared to answer these questions, so he went on and on, and talked about the courage it took to move to Bosnia, "the wild frontier of the Austro-Hungarian empire." He dwelt for some time, as I was successfully resisting retching, on "the progress that we brought to these parts" with "civilized beekeeping, iron plough and carpentry skills." We built "our empire out of nothing," and it was "no accident that our grandfather met with the Archduke before he was assassinated—our stock is heroic and royal." He told us (although I was barely there) that we should "read the Greeks, the founders of the Western civilization" if we didn't believe him—"We're all over the history of literature." So he proliferated thoughts about the family history, mentioning names that I could not attach to faces anymore—they all merged into my grandfather who was presently and perpetually passing in and out of nothingness. I do not know where our greatness

ended—if it indeed ever ended—for I passed out. Then I
heard an energetic applause, a choir of hands clapping and
clapping, and someone was slapping my face. As I opened my
eyes, everything rushed away from me, except the face of my
mother, who said: "It seems that the history wore you out. Do
you want to vomit?"

My mother led me away, while I mismanaged my steps,
from the tumultuous tribal space, holding my right arm above
the elbow, and I felt her swollen, arthritic knuckles squeezing
my muscle. "The trouble with the Hemons," she said, "is that
they always get much too excited about things they imagine to
be real." I was wobbling, looking at the prows of my feet,
imagining the straight line that I had to follow so as not to appear drunk. But then I simply closed my eyes and let my
mother steer me around chairs and chickens and buckets and
tree stumps and flower beds.

"I made a terrible fool of myself," I said.

"You're almost a man now," she said. "And that is a man's
privilege."

She made me sit under a shriveled apple tree. Small, wiz-
ened apples—not unlike my brain at the moment—hung like
earrings from crooked, exhausted branches. My mother sat
down by my side and put her arm around me. I wanted to put
my head into her lap, but she said: "No, you'll just get dizzier."

We could hear the Hemons-Hemuns hollering against the
music, which from a distance sounded discordant. We could
still hear the trucks and I vaguely realized that they had been
passing by all day. "I wish these trucks would stop," I said.

"They probably won't for a while," my mother said. Her
hands smelled of coffee and vanilla sugar. She told me about
the time her father gave their only horse away.

"It was in forty-three or forty-four, a young man came running out of the corn. Mother and Father knew him, he was lanky and had blue eyes, a Muslim from a nearby village. He said that the Chetniks had killed his whole family, that he escaped by leaping through a window and now they were after him. He had a bruise on his cheek, as if someone had kissed him with plum-lips. He asked my father for the horse so he could get away and join the partisans. Father glanced at my mother, she said nothing, but he knew and he went to get the horse, cursing all along: 'Fuck this world and the bloody sun and this country when everyone needs my horse.' The young man, his name was Zaim, kissed both of my father's cheeks and promised he would return the horse once the evil had blown over. So he rode off, waving at us. But then the Chetniks came riding their horses, like cowboys. 'Where is he?' they yelled. 'Where's the circumcised dog?' And my father says: 'What's the trouble, brothers?' They all have beards and rifles and knives, they shout: 'Did you see the Turkish bastard?' Father says: 'I don't know who you're talking about.' 'You're lying!' they yell. 'You're a traitor!' Then they beat him with rifle butts, they throw him on the ground and kick him with their boots. 'What's wrong with you, motherfucker, you're one of us! Where's the Turk? Who's he to you?' I thought they would slit our throats, no problem. My brother was in the partisans, but we spread the word that he was in Srem, working."

"You've never told me this," I said.

She continued: "They kept beating him until he was bleeding and unconscious. My mother wept and begged them to spare him. Then one of them, beardless, came to me and said: 'There's a little Serbian girl who is going to tell us where the Turk is.' Oh, I couldn't say a word, and then I saw my mother's eyes, frightened, and her hands squeezing the strength out of each other. I told them I didn't see anyone and that I would tell them if I did. So they left, and the beardless one told us that he would personally judge us if he found out we were lying. That was our only horse, you know, all we had."

I resisted falling asleep, trying to keep my eyes open, but then I succumbed, leaning on my mother's shoulder, even in my dreams aware of the possibility of disgorging myself. I slept for hours, thinking in my troublesome sleep that I was leaning on my mother, but then I woke up, with my cheek on a molehill, sprawled on the ground which was covered with rotting apples. I went back to the yard and all the Hemuns were gone, as if I had dreamt them; and everyone else, scattered around, was cleaning up, storing away the food or taking the tent and the stage apart. I need not have been there to know what happened at the end. It could all be seen on the tape, which we occasionally watch when I visit my parents in Schaumburg, Illinois. We rewind and fast-forward, to get to the moment we most want to cherish. We freeze the frame to remember a name, we fill in the gaps, caused by unwarranted cuts and blanks due to a ten-dollar conversion in a Pakistani store on Devon. Frequently, there's a little tide of fractious dots rising from the bottom of a trembling picture, always trying to reach the center. Finally, the last image is of my mother, just about to say something—something irreverent about "the Hemon propaganda," perhaps. That is all too clear from her clever eyes and the lingering, undeveloped grin. She never says it, forever on the verge of saying something. She can never remember what she was going to say, and the screen suddenly turns blindingly blue, and we turn it off and rewind the tape to the beginning.

A COIN

FOR ZRINKA

Suppose there is a Point A and a Point B and that, if you want
to get from point A to point B, you have to pass through an
open space clearly visible to a skillful sniper. You have to run
from Point A to Point B and the faster you run, the more likely
you are to reach Point B alive. The space between Point A and
Point B is littered with things that sprinting citizens dropped
along the way. A black leather wallet, probably empty. A purse,
agape like a mouth. A white plastic water vessel, with a bullet
hole in its center. A green-red-brown shawl ornamented with
snowflakes, dirty. A wet loaf of bread, with busy ants crawling
all over it, as if building a pyramid. A videocassette, dismem-
bered, several of its pieces still connected with a dark writhing
tape. On days when snipers are particularly rabid, there are
scattered bodies as well. Some of them may still be alive and
twitching toward the distant cover, leaving a bloody trail behind, like snails. People seldom try to help them, for everybody
knows that the snipers are just waiting for that. Sometimes a
sniper mercifully finishes off the crawling person. Sometimes
the snipers play with the body, shooting off his or her knees,
feet, or elbows. They seem to have made a bet how far he or
she is going to get before bleeding away.

Sarajevo is a catless city. It is so because people couldn't
feed them, or couldn't take them along when they were fleeing, or their owners were killed. Hence the dogs that couldn't
be fed or taken along hunt them down and devour them. One
can often see, among the rubble on the streets, underneath

burnt cars, or stuck in sewers, cat carcasses, or cat heads with a
death grin, eye-teeth like miniature daggers. Sometimes one
can see two or more dogs fighting over a cat, tearing apart a
screaming loaf of fur and flesh.

*Aida's letters are scarce and sudden, escaping the siege via UN
convoys, foreign reporters, or refugee transports. I imagine them in a
sack, in the back of a UN truck, driven by a Pakistani or Ukrainian
soldier oblivious to everything but the muddy road before him and the
gaze of the bearded thugs by the road, their index fingers conspicu-
ously close to the trigger; or a letter in a reporter's bag carelessly
thrown over a tattooed shoulder, sharing the bottom of the bag with a
Walkman, notebooks, condoms, bread and pot crumbs, and a wallet
crammed with family pictures. I imagine letters in a post office in Zagreb or Split, Amsterdam or London, in the midst of a pile of letters
sent to people I know nothing about by the people who care about them.
Sometimes it takes dismal months for her letters to reach me and when
I open my mailbox—a long tunnel dead-ending with a dark square—
and find Aida's letter, I shiver with dread. What terrifies me is that, as
I rip the exhausted envelope, she may be dead. She may have vanished,
may have already become a ghost, a nothing—a fictitious character, so
to speak—and I'm reading her letter as if she were alive, her voice
ringing in my brain, her visions projected before my eyes, her hand
shaping curved letters. I fear to communicate with a creature of my
memory, with a dead person. I dread the fact that life is always slower
than death and I have been chosen, despite my weakness, against my
will, to witness the discrepancy.*

In September, Aunt Fatima passed away. She had had
asthma for a long time, but in September she just asphyxiated
in our apartment. They were pouring shells for weeks on end,
and even when they didn't there was an eager sniper. He killed

our neighbor who hadn't even left the building. He just peeked out of the door, cautiously ajar, and the bullet hit him in the forehead and he just dropped down dead. Anyway, Aunt Fatima ran out of her asthma medicine, and she couldn't go out. The windows had been shattered long ago. She was always cold, breathing in cold air saturated with floating dust and hovering particles of rubble. She simply suffocated, producing that inhaling, sucking sound, and nothing was being inhaled. We couldn't bury her, or even take her out, because they kept shelling and sniping as if there was no tomorrow.

Kevin is an American, from Chicago. He's a cameraman. He's been around, he says. He's been in Afghanistan and Lebanon and the Persian Gulf and Africa with his camera. He's tall, his arms are little hills of muscles. His eyes are greenish, like dried turf. He has two parallel silver earrings in his left ear. His hair is short. He's balding and has a peninsula of grayish hair crawling down his forehead. He's lean. When you look closely, you can see purple ruptured blood vessels where his nose meets his face. It's from cocaine. He did it a lot in Lebanon. It was cheap and he broke down. He couldn't stand it any longer. An Arab child shot at him with what he took to be a toy gun. There is a scar-furrow on his thigh. He was new, he broke down, he did cocaine. Now he's fine, he says. I like him because he tells stories. All of those people do, all those reporters and cameramen and all those who have been around. But they're all clichés, as if they watched too many movies about foreign correspondents and war reporters. Kevin's stories are different. All those others always tell stories about other journalists. A British drunk, a German ex-Nazi, a French sissy, an American whore, are stock characters. They never tell stories about the local people, because the natives are news, they're what's to be reported.

Kevin told me stories from Afghanistan, about lying in a high mountain ambush with bearded rebels. And about terrified Russian convoys crawling up a dire mountain road, knowing they're being watched. About a Russian soldier being cut in pieces alive, producing unreal shrieks, until a merciful *mullah* shot him in the head. He filmed it, even though he knew they would take the tape away from him. Even if they didn't, it would have never been broadcast.

She sent me a black-and-white picture: she is standing on a pile of debris in the midst of the Library ruins. I could see holes that used to be windows, and pillars like scorched matches. The camera looks at her from underneath: she is tall and erect, as if on the top of a mountain; she is in a bulletproof vest, wearing it detachedly, as though it were a bathing suit.

I've got this job as a liaison for the pool of foreign TV companies. Besides helping them to get by in hell, to approach and bribe government officials and find good parties, I edit footage that crews shoot in and around the city. Then I send it via satellite to London, Amsterdam, Luxembourg, or wherever. I get two–three hours of footage every day. It's mainly blood and gore and severed limbs. I cut it into fifteen–twenty minutes, which are then transmitted to the invisible people who edit it into one–two minutes of a news story, if there is one. At the beginning, I was trying to choose the most telling images, with as much blood and bowels, stumps and child corpses as possible. I was trying to induce some compassion or understanding or pain or whatever, although the one–two minutes that I would later recognize as having been cut by me would contain only mildly horrific images. I've changed my view. I stopped sifting horror after I saw footage of a dead woman being carried by four men. She was prone on their arms, as if on a hearse. As they were carrying her, her head was bent backward, hanging down. Her skull was cut open by a piece of shrapnel. There was a skull-sod with hair, hanging on a patch of skin. They put her in the back of a truck, with other heaped corpses. Her head was still open. I could see the brainless bloody cavity. Then one of the men closed the cavity, putting the sod back into its place, as if putting on a lid. He did it with a certain reluctant respect, as though he was covering her naked body, as though there was something indecent in seeing the inside of somebody's head. I cut all that out and put it on a separate tape. From then on I was cutting out everything that was as horrid. I put it all on one tape, which I hoarded underneath my pillow made of clothes. There once was that corny idiotic movie *Cinema Paradiso,* where the projectionist kept all the kisses from films censored by a priest. Hence I christened the tape *Cinema Inferno.* I haven't watched it entirely yet. Some day I will, paying particular attention to the cuts, to see how the montage of death attractions works.

I had a dream: a woman alone on the glowing screen, and a moat in front of it, and beyond the moat is a room, windowless, full of people. She is performing me, she is acting me out. I'm in the audience, sitting in a row at the end of my gaze, on the verge of darkness. She's not doing it right. This is not how I felt, this is not my pain. I want to get up and scream, and tell her that she's much too involved in myself. She's even attaining my shapes, my face, my voice. I want to help her step out of me. But I can't do anything. She's a light mirage. I can't get up, because I don't know what exactly is wrong. And then I realize—it's the language. I'm confined within the wrong language.

Purebred dogs can be seen running in packs or, seldom, alone. You can see German shepherds, Irish setters, Belgian collies, Border collies, rottweilers, poodles, chow chows, Dobermans, cocker spaniels, malamutes, Siberian huskies, everything. After years of siege, there are, naturally, many mongrels. Some of the breeding combinations would amaze, or terrify, a canine expert. In the winter, when every living creature is in the middle of starvation, dogs are more inclined to move in packs, often attacking with common strategy, like wolves. There have been occasions when an improbable mixture of dog races attacked a child or a feeble elderly person. A German shepherd would be going for the throat, a poodle would be tearing the flesh off the calves.

It is after I write her a letter with trite reminiscing that I begin wanting to tell her all about me—I have imaginary conversations with her, making real grimaces, gesturing with real hands. I think of all the things I could've told her or should've told her: how awkward and cumbersome I feel in English, sinking in syntax, my sentences flapping helplessly, like a drowning child's arms; about Bach's St. Matthew's Passion; *about hoping for the arrival of spiders—the vicious cockroach-killers—into my living space; about the lack of relationship—or contact, rather—with women; about the friendless immigrant life; about the* Headline News *I keep watching, waiting for a glimpse of Sarajevo; about my western window, looking at corny sunsets and the distant O'Hare Airport, night airplanes landing like tired firebugs; about an involuntary memory I had about my father smashing a nest of infant mice with a shovel; about the fact that almost everything I wanted to tell her is not in the letter; about the sense of loss and the damp stamp-glue taste lingering on my tongue for hours after I drop the letter in the mailbox. I used to believe that words can convey and contain everything, but not anymore, not anymore.*

I grew fond of Kevin because he never openly showed me his affection. He would just tell me stories. Even in a room full of people, I knew the stories were for me. I liked him because he was so detached. He said it was the "cameraman syndrome," always being a gaze away from the world. We're not in love, love is out of the question. Nobody's in love in this godforsaken city. We just keep learning about each other. We just share stories, becoming a story along the way. And the story may end at any moment. When we make love, in the darkness—no electricity—it's harsh and cruel, as if we were fighting, because we have to wrestle joy and flashes of love from our irked bodies. We never talk about his future departure. He has callused feet, from marching through the Afghanistan mountains.

After some grotesque obsequies, we put Aunt Fatima in my room. It soon became *her* room. None of us would go in there. When something was needed from her room—a scarf, a blanket, a photo—someone would say: "It's in Fatima's room," which meant it was irretrievable. We kept hoping that we would be able to bury her, but a week passed and she was still there—my malodorous aunt.

On Tuesday I had a sensation (a hallucination?) of cockroaches scurrying up my shins—I may be losing my mind, because of the solitude and nothingness that constitute my life. I had the sensation at a rock show, while boys and girls shook their heads like rattles. I thought that the cockroaches were my home-grown cockroaches, that I brought them with me from my apartment, unknowingly. The next day I asked Art, my janitor, to help me and he gave me those roach motels in which roaches get lured by sweet syrup and then get stuck in glue. Let's put it this way: Art provides room for abhorrent insects, Art terminates cockroaches.

I hate Kevin. He brought footage of yet another massacre: people crawling in their own blood, faceless skulls, limbs strewn, stuff like that. There was this woman, her arms were severed. You could see two frayed, blood-spurting stumps. She was raising the bloody mess of her ex-arms toward Kevin's camera. Kevin had a close-up of her face, still in shock, not feeling any pain, not being armless yet. The close-up lasted for a good five minutes, like fucking Tarkovsky. I asked Kevin why he didn't drop the goddamn camera and help the woman. He said there was nothing he could do. He's a cameraman, he said, and that is what he does and how he helps people. I told him he shouldn't have shot that close-up. He said he didn't do it. It was his camera who did it, he just held it. I cut it out anyway. I put it on the *Cinema Inferno* tape. Nobody saw the footage but me. Kevin is so detached and so protected.

I sleep in a former TV studio, next to the editing room. It is windowless, of course, safe from shelling, unless they use concrete-piercing shells. Which they seldom do, for whatever reason. I suppose that even such a shell wouldn't kill us immediately. It would just open a hole for more shells. I prefer to die immediately. The studio has a little stage where mindless folk singers used to perform their playback love pain. This is where we sleep, as if on a raft—on a stage soaked with false tears and real sweat. There are still several cameras in the studio, with their lenses turned to the floor, looking between their wheels, as if ashamed. The studio is immense and very dark. We light it with two strategically positioned candles. There is some electricity in the building, to be sure, produced by a coughing gasoline-run generator, but we need electricity to produce and broadcast images. We move around the studio as if blind, having a memory of the studio as the map in our heads. We never move cameras, lest we run into them and get hurt. But some-how they always get in our way, as if they're moving silently behind our backs, like ghosts, recording us.

I've been sending letters for her through obscure Red Cross chan-nels—it takes months for a Red Cross convoy to reach Sarajevo and even more for my letters to reach her. When they do, they're already obsolete, they're rendering someone other than myself, someone saner—a stranger not only to her but indeed to myself. When I'm writ-ing those letters I have to accept my helplessness, I have to admit that someone else is writing them, using my body, my Pelikan fountain pen, my cramped right hand. Whatever I write, I feel it to be untrue, because it'll be untrue in a day or two, if not in a moment or two. Whatever I say I am lying or will be lying. On the pages of the letter, the whiteness of the page stained with ink, a dismal present descends into a desolate past. That is why I tend to write her things that she al-ready knows, tell her stories told wars ago. It is cowardly, I confess, but I'm just trying to create an illusion that our lives, however distant, may still be simultaneous.

The odor escaped Fatima's room no matter what we tried to do. We stuffed the cracks between the door and the frame with rugs. We soaked the rugs and the door with vinegar and our useless perfumes (Obsession, Magie Noir). But the stench was always there—the sweet, dense, meaty scent of decay. In the midst of a rare and brief nocturnal lull in shelling, we de-cided to throw her out of the window, after my mother woke up screaming, having dreamt maggots coming out of her sis-ter's eye sockets.

Kevin and I, we get drunk over his stories, with bourbon that he keeps fetching from somewhere. He tells me then what he considers to be intimate things: about his long-time girl-friend, who was working as a real estate agent, having a dream of becoming a congresswoman. She was from a place called White Pigeon, Michigan, fifty miles south of Kalamazoo. While he was in the Gulf, she left him a message on his an-swering machine about leaving him because he was a "selfish dreamy idiot." He tells me how he sees everything through a viewfinder. He has confidence in the camera objective. He feels natural with his camera, because "with the camera I see nothing alone." There's always another pair of eyes, he says.

A friend of mine asked me to help her identify some damaged buildings in Sarajevo; she sent me photographs hoping that I could rec-ognize the buildings, but they were unidentifiable as far as I was con-cerned. They all looked the same: they all had shattered windows—black holes, as if their eyes had been gouged; there were rings of debris around them, as if ruins were being carved out of whole build-ings; there were no people in the pictures. What was in the pictures were not buildings—let alone buildings I could've come in or out of: what was in the pictures was what was not in the pictures—the pictures recorded the very end of the process of disappearing, the nothingness itself.

People stand in line at Point A, waiting for their turn to run across. When it's your turn, you cannot wait, you have to go, because the longer you wait, the readier the sniper is. Plus you don't want to share the unspeakable fear of the waiting throng. The first time I ran from Point A to Point B, the fear was unspeakable indeed. Pain in your stomach, as if a big steel ball is grinding your bowels. Blood throbbing in your neck veins. Wet heat inside your eyeballs. Numbness of your limbs, increasing as you're running. Sweat trickling down your cheeks, like a miniature avalanche of dread. You see no life unwinding before your eyes. All you see is one or two meters ahead of you and all the little things that you can trip over. You hear every tiny sound. Your feet brushing away dirt and rubble. Distant detonations. Cries of scared and wounded people. Whistling ricocheting bullets. The death rattle from the person behind you.

This is me in what's left of the Library. If you could magnify this picture sufficiently you would see motes levitating around me—cold ashes of books. This picture was made on the day I got the bulletproof vest. It was one of the happiest days of my life, this life. A bulletproof vest significantly increases your (well, mine) chances of survival. The sniper has to shoot you in the head to kill you. Which is why I cut my hair so short, to make my head smaller. Sometimes I feel like a fucking Joan of Arc, except I have no army and no voices to guide me.

Mother and Father wrapped her up in a bedsheet, and then another one, and then another one, their faces distorted by the urge to vomit. I couldn't watch when they actually pushed her over the windowsill, but I heard the thud. I thought, as if remembering a line from a movie: "Her life ended with a thud."

Since April I have received no letters from Aida. From that time on I had to make up her letters, I had to write her letters for her, I had to imagine her, because that was the only way to break the siege and stay connected with her. I'm sure she's alive, I'm sure that one of these days I'll have a bundle of her consecutive letters stowed in my mailbox, I'm sure she's writing them this very moment.

This war, my friend, is men's business. The other day I heard a "joke": "What is a woman?"—"The stuff around the pussy!" The men in the camouflage uniforms thought it was so hilarious that they kicked the floor with their rifle butts. I sensed that the joke was for me. We're expected to remain silent, spread our legs, breed more warriors, and die with motherly dignity. I think what I fear the most is rape. When a sniper bullet hits you, your body and yourself die simultaneously. Provided, naturally, that you're killed instantly; which you usually are, because they're so fucking good. But I don't want my body to be mutilated, mauled, violated. I don't want to witness that. When I'm gone I'd like to take my body with me. Have you heard about the rape camps?

When I got this job, I moved to the TV building, going home only occasionally, to check if my parents were alive and well. I'd usually go on Sunday afternoons, after the morning transmission of Friday leftovers. But then I stopped doing that because I realized that my local sniper was waiting for me. Before I ran, everything was silent, and several people ran across the parking lot without being shot at. When I started crossing it, bullets buzzed around me like rabid bees. He watched me. He knew I was coming. He waited for me and then toyed with me. Now I go to see them at different times, using different routes, trying to appear differently each time in order to be unrecognizable to the sharpshooter, who could be one of my ex-boyfriends for all I know.

While my head was still on the pillow, my nightmare not completely erased by the sudden awakening, I opened my eyes and saw a cockroach running from the stove, over the gray kitchen-floor tiles, getting on the carpet, running a bit slower, as if on sand, going beneath

the chair, coming diagonally across, going around my slippers, trying
to reach the safe space underneath my futon. I watched it, it was run-
ning fast, never stopping, going straight without hesitation. What was
it running from? What was running that little engine? Desire to live?
Fear of death? The instinctual—perhaps, even, molecular—aware-
ness of the gaze of the supreme sharpshooter? What a horrible world,
I thought, when every living creature lives and dies in fear. I reached
for my left slipper, but the cockroach was already underneath the
futon.

Snipers often kill dogs, just for fun. Sometimes they have competitions in dog-shooting, but only when there aren't any targetable people on the streets. Shooting a dog in the head gets you the most points, I suppose. One can often see a dog corpse with a shattered head, like a crushed tomato. When snipers shoot dogs, antisniping patrols refrain from confronting them, because of the constant danger of a rabies epidemic. When an unskilled, new, or careless sharpshooter only wounds a dog and the dog frantically ricochets around, bleeding, howling, biting anything that can ease the pain and fear, a member of the antisniping patrol might even shoot the dog, aiming, as always, at the head.

The other day I took Kevin to a tour of my favorite places in Sarajevo. He took his camera. What I like about Kevin is that you don't have to explain everything to him. He just sees what you want him to see. What's more, he doesn't say that he understands. You just know. We both knew, for instance, that the places on our tour were between being a memory and being reduced to nothing but a pile of rubble. The camera was recording the process of disappearing. There is a truce in place these days, which always scares me a bit. Partly because silence is often more terrifying than the familiar relentless noise of shelling. Partly because I'm afraid that Kevin might get bored and leave. Which is why, I suppose, I took him on the tour. He followed me with his camera like a shadow. I showed him our school. I stood in the wrecked window of our classroom and he shot me waving to his objective. I stood on the corner from which Princip shot those historic shots. My little feet were fitting, as always, into the concrete shapes of his feet. I took him to the few bars we used to frequent. Some of them were closed—the owner dead or something—and some of them were full of black marketers and men in uniform, their rifles conspicuous on the bar-stand before them. I took him to the park, now treeless—desperate firewood demand—where I used to take boys and make them touch my breasts, while they were being too pusillanimous to go further. I told all that to the camera, and he circled around me, his knees bent, as if genuflecting. And then I told him, as I am telling the invisible you now, that I was pregnant.

Then we watched over it, the white pile that used to be my aunt, from the window that was hidden from snipers. We watched the bundle of decomposed flesh, as if we were on a wake, but a wake for something other than Aunt Fatima, and transcendentally important nonetheless. We would take turns, we would have shifts. Father even asked me, taking his shift, if everything was all right. I said: "No, nothing will ever be all right." I'm terrified with the calmness, even if ostensible, with which I'm telling you this. I feel I might burst out into madness.

In the corners of my room, there are elaborate cobwebs, but I haven't seen any spiders. It seems that the cobwebs have a purely sym-

bolic function—they're there to remind me that I am trapped and that, at any given moment, a tooth or a sting will inject poison into my body and then suck out my blood. The space I inhabit becomes me—the room speaks about me, as if the walls were pages of a book and I were a hero, a character, somebody.

So I had the morning shift. And right after it dawned, I saw a pack of dogs coming toward us. There was a rottweiler, a poodle, and several mongrels. They tore the sheets and I turned my head away, but I could not leave. The only thought I remember having was about skiing. I had a vision of myself coming down the slope, going very fast, and air slapping my cheeks, and the sound of the skis brushing snow away, like a speeded-up recording of waves. When I looked out again, I couldn't look at the place where the corpse was. I looked around it, as if making a compromise. I saw the rottweiler, trotting away, with a hand in his jaw. I wish I'd had a camera so I wouldn't have to remember. I'm sorry I had to tell you this.

My hair is all gray now. How is Chicago? Write, even if your letters can't reach me.

With a lightning move of my hand superbly handling the knife, I split the cockroach in two: the front half continued running for an inch or two and then started frenetically revolving around the head; the back half just stood in place, as if surprised, oozing pallid slime.

I woke up bleeding, in a bed soaked with blood, by the Heathrow Airport, in an expensive bland hotel, having waited for Kevin for more than a week. Kevin, who didn't even bother to call me. I tried to reach him in Amsterdam, Paris, Atlanta, New York, Cyprus, even Johannesburg, leaving messages and curses. But then I just wiped myself off and went back to Sarajevo, leaving a heap of bloody towels and bedsheets, an empty refreshment bar, a broken glass in the bathroom, and an unpaid bill, to Kevin's name, with his Cyprus address. So here I am now, un-pregnant, as sanguine as ever, but never as sad.

I bought a Polaroid camera to explore my absence, to find out how space and things appear when I'm not exerting my presence on them. I took snapshots—glossy still moments with edges darker than the center, as if everything is fading away—I took snapshots of my apartment and the things in it: here's my ceiling fan not revolving; here's my empty chair; here's my futon, looking like somebody's just got up; here's my vacuous bathroom; here's a dried cockroach; here's a glass, with still water not being drunk; here are my vacant shoes; here's my TV not being watched; here's a flash in the mirror; here's nothing.

When you get to Point B, the adrenaline rush is so strong that you feel *too* alive. You see everything clearly, but you can't comprehend anything. Your senses are so overloaded that you forget everything before you even register it. I've run from Point A to Point B hundreds of times and the feeling is always the same but I've never had it before. I suppose it is this high pressure of excitement that makes people bleed away so quickly. I saw deluges of blood coming out of svelte bodies. A woman holding on to her purse while her whole body is shaking with death rattle. I saw bloodstreams spouting out of surprised children, and they look at you as if they'd done something wrong—broken a vial of expensive perfume or something. But once you get to Point B everything is quickly gone, as if it never happened. You pick yourself up and walk back into your besieged life, happy to be. You move a wet curl from your forehead, inhale deeply, and put your hand in the pocket, where you may or may not find a worthless coin; a coin.

BLIND JOZEF PRONEK

&

DEAD SOULS

And, finally, when after sneaking from dresser to closet, he had found piece by piece all he needed and had finished his dressing among the furniture which bore with him in silence, and was ready at last, he stood, hat in hand, feeling rather embarrassed that even at the last moment he could not find a word which would dispel that hostile silence; he then walked toward the door slowly, resignedly, hanging his head, while someone else, someone forever turning his back, walked at the same pace in the opposite direction into the depths of the mirror, through the row of empty rooms which did not exist.

—BRUNO SCHULZ,
Mr. Charles

FOR
SEMEZDIN MEHMEDINOVIC

The Red Scarf

As soon as Pronek stepped out of the plane (an exhausted steward, crumpled and hoary, beamed an "Auf Wiedersehen" at him), he realized that he had left his red wool scarf in the luggage compartment, with a mustard stain from the Vienna airport café. He contemplated going back to fetch it, but the relentless piston of his fellow pilgrims pushed him through the mazy tunnel, until he saw a line of booths echoing one another, with uniformed officers lodged in them reading little passport books, as sundry passengers waited obediently behind a thick yellow line on the floor. There was a man holding a sign with Pronek's name misspelled on it (Proniek), monitoring the throng winding between black ribbons, as if the man were choosing a person to attach the name to. Pronek walked up to him and said: "I am that person." "Oh, you are," the man said. "Welcome to the States."

"Thank you," Pronek said. "Thank you very much."

The man led him past the passels of people clutching passports, pushing their tumescent handbags with their feet. "We don't have to wait," he said, nodding at Pronek for some reason, as if conveying a secret message. "You're our guest."

"Thank you!" Pronek said.

The man took him up to the booth filled to the glass-pane brim with a gigantic man. Had someone abruptly opened the door of his booth, his flesh would have oozed out slowly, Pronek thought, like runny dough.

"Hi, Wyatt!" said Pronek's guide.

"Hi, Virgil!" said the dough man.

"He's our guest!" said Virgil.

"How're you doin', buddy?" said the dough man. He was mustached, and suddenly Pronek realized that he resembled the fat detective with a loose tie and an unbuttoned shirt from an American TV show.

"I'm very well, sir, I thank you very much," Pronek said.

"Wha're you goin' to do here, buddy?"

"I do not know right now, sir. Travel. I think they have program for me."

"I'm sure they do," he said, flipping through Pronek's red Yugoslav passport, as if it were a gooey smut magazine. Then he grabbed a stamp and violently slammed it against a passport page and said: "You have a hell of a time, y'hear now, buddy."

"I will, sir. Thank you very much."

What we have just seen is Jozef Pronek entering the United States of America. It was January 26, 1992. Once he found himself on this side, he didn't feel anything different. He knew full well, however, he couldn't go back to retrieve his red scarf with the yellow mustard stamp.

Virgil began explaining to Pronek how to get on the plane to Washington, D.C., but Pronek wasn't really listening, for Virgil's spectacular head suddenly became visible to him. He saw the valley of baldness between the two tufts of hair, stretching away in horror from the emerging globe. The skin of Virgil's face was inscribed with an intricate network of blood vessels, like river systems on a map, with two crimson deltas around his nostrils. Hair was peering out of his nose, swaying almost imperceptibly, as if a couple of centipedes were stuck in his nostrils, hopelessly moving their little legs. Pronek didn't know what Virgil was saying, but still kept saying: "I know. I know." Then Virgil generously shook Pronek's hand and said: "We're so happy to have you here." What could Pronek say? He said: "Thank you."

He exchanged money with a listless carbuncular teenager behind a thick glass pane, and obediently sat down at a bar that invited him with a glaring neon sign: "Have a drink with us." He was reading dollar bills ("In God we trust") when the waitress said: "They're pretty green, ahn't they? Wha' canna gechou, honey?"

"Beer," Pronek said.

"What kinda beer? This is not Russia, hun, we got all kindsa beer. We got Michelob, Milleh, Milleh Lite, Milleh Genuine Draft, Bud, Bud Light, Bud Ice. Wha'ever you want."

She brought him a Bud (Light) and asked: "What's your team in the Superbawl?"

"I don't know."

"I'm a Buffalo girl. I'm just gonna die if the Bills lose again."

"I hope they won't," he said.

"They better not," she said. "Or I be real mad."

All the TVs in the bar were on, but the images were distorted. The square heads of two toupeed men talking were winding upward like smoke, then they would straighten up, and Pronek could see them grinning at their microphones, as if they were delectable lollipops, then they would twist again. He thought, for a moment, that his eyes were not adjusted to the ways in which images were transmitted in this country. He remembered that dogs saw everything differently from people and that everything looked dim to them. Not to mention bats, which couldn't even see a thing, but flew around, bumping into telephone poles, with something like a sonar in their heads, which meant that they understood only echoes.

This is the kind of profitless thought that Pronek frequently had.

Pronek saw an elderly couple sitting down under one of the TVs. The man had wrinkles emerging, like rays, from the corners of his eyes, and a Redskins hat. The woman had puffed-up hair, and she looked a lot like the Washington on the one-dollar bill. A sign behind their backs said "Smoking Section." They sat silent; their gazes, perpendicular to each other, converged over the tin ashtray in the center of the table. The waitress ("I'm Grace," she said. "How's everything?") brought them two Miller Lites, but they didn't touch them. Instead, the man took a black book out of his worn-out canvas handbag and spread it between the two sweating bottles. Then they read it together, their heads nearly touching, the man's left hand heaped upon the woman's right hand, like a frog upon a frog making love. They started weeping, squeezing each other's hands so hard that Pronek could see the woman's finger tips reddening, while her pink nails seemed to be stretching out.

This was, for Pronek, the first in the series of what we normally call culture shocks.

He roved all over the airport, imagining that it had the shape of John Kennedy's supine body, with his legs and arms outstretched, and leech-like airplanes sucking its toes and fingers. He imagined traveling through Kennedy's digestive system, swimming in a bubbling river of acid, like bacteria, and ending up in his gurgling kidney-bathroom. He stepped out of the airport through one of JFK's nostrils, in front of which there were cabs lined up like a thin mustache.

Finally, he joined the line of people trickling into the tunnel to the Washington, D.C., plane. "How are you today?" said a steward, not bothering to hear the answer. Pronek had a window seat, and a man who looked as if he had just been attached to an air compressor, like a balloon, sat next to him—

the man was so fat that he occupied two seats and had to buckle his left thigh.

"Can't believe I am missing the Super Bowl," the man said and exhaled. "I went to every goddamn Redskins game this year and I had to miss the biggie. The fucking biggie. Are you a Redskins fan?"

"I'm afraid I don't even know the rules of the game."

"Ah, you're a foreigner!" he triumphantly exclaimed and exhaled again. "What do you think of America? Isn't it the greatest country on earth?"

"I'm afraid I don't know yet. I just arrived."

"It's great. People are great. Freedom, all that. Best in the world." He concluded the conversation with an authoritative head twitch, and opened a book entitled *Seven Spiritual Laws of Growth.* Pronek looked out at the aluminum sternness of the wing, his body twisted, his cheek against the seat texture, whose chaffing reminded him of his red scarf, and then he fell asleep, until the ascendance of his guts to his throat, as the plane was taking off, woke him up.

Marbles

Pronek hated his neck, because it always got stiff and became a knot of thick sinews. He would keep pressing them, which would just produce more and more pain, while the sinews would wiggle under his fingers, as hard as steel cables. If he ever were to be decapitated, he thought, the executioner would be in danger, for the ax would probably bounce back and split the poor fellow's head like a watermelon. They would have to soak his neck in acid for a week or so, in order to soften the steely sinews, and then cut off his head.

Pronek and his umbrous co-passengers descended upon Washington, and he had to turn his whole body to look through the window at the feeble capital lights, "like moribund embers under the ashes of a cloudy night" (this was Pronek's thought at the moment, and we must concede it is rather nice). The flight attendant sneaked from somewhere behind Pronek's back and startled him, shoving his face in the crevice between the fat man's chest and the seat in front of him, and asking: "Can I get you another beer, sir?" Pronek turned his whole body—the sinews resisting painfully—like a hand puppet, toward the attendant and allowed him to provide more helpful service. The attendant seemed to be paid per smile and had the tan of an impeccably baked chicken.

Pronek was pushed into the airport building by the piston of his fellow pilgrims, as described before.

First the gigantic tip of a nipple on a stick started flashing and hooting, then the empty carousel started revolving. Bulky bags and square suitcases began dropping out from behind the black curtain, then went—wooo!—down the slide into the immutability of the carousel's revolution. Pronek's faceless co-passengers swarmed around the carousel, as if they were bacteria at the bottom of a stomach, and the food to be digested was just being sent from the oral department. Pronek's bag was lost. He stared at the empty carousel, which revolved meaninglessly until it stopped to shine in conspicuous silence. Pronek had only a handbag packed with books and duty-free shop catalogs, plus a piece of three-day-old bourek, designed by his mother to sustain him on the trip, which was now—we can be sure of that—breeding all kinds of belligerent Balkan microorganisms.

Behind a frail, black, and long ribbon, there stood a man with Pronek's name (misspelled as "Pronak"), followed by a question mark. The man held it out just above his pelvis, with the lower edge cutting gently into the palms of his hands, so Pronek thought that his name had been taken away from him and given to this man, who was obviously an honest, hard-working, disciplined individual. The man shook Pronek's flaccid hand hesitantly, as if afraid that the sign might be taken away from him.

The man welcomed Pronek and asked about the trip with fake—but clearly polite—interest. "It was like Marlow's journey to see Kurtz," Pronek said. "Wow!" said the man, doubtless unaware of what Pronek was talking about—for which he shouldn't be blamed. The man had dark, short hair, retreating in disarray from his forehead, with ashen smudges behind his ears. He kindly helped Pronek inquire about the luggage, but to no avail.

Outside, it was snowing relentlessly, as if the ireful God was tearing up down pillows in the heavens. The man drove through the blindingly white maze of the blizzard. He pointed at objects and buildings, which kept popping out of tumultuous snow like jacks-in-the-box: a gigantic toothpick, lit from below, as if kneeling worshippers were pointing flashlights at its pinnacle; a series of buildings that Pronek decided to describe in future conversations with whomever was interested in his U.S. impressions as built in a neo-Nazi, neo-classical, neo-fluffy style (which is not entirely justified, we believe).

"And this is the White House," the man said, exultantly.

"I always wandered," Pronek said, incorrectly. "Why it is called White House? Do you have to be white to live there?"

The man did not find it amusing, so he said: "No, it is because it is made of white marble."

Pronek's neck was stiffer than ever, at this point practically petrified, so he turned his whole body toward the man and put his left hand on the head-recliner behind the man's nape, which shamelessly sported tufts of unruly hair. The man glanced at Pronek's hand, as if afraid that it might choke him.

"Did they use slaves to build it?"

"I don't know, but I don't believe so."

The man's name was Simon.

They drove in silence, as the storm was subsiding. By the time they got to the hotel, leafy snowflakes were butterflying, taking a break after a hard day's work. Simon complimented Pronek's English, and—having established a bond, presumably—informed him that the Redskins had won. "I barely know rules," Pronek retorted. "It's a great game," Simon said, and then invited him to his home in Falls Orchard, Virginia, to meet his wife, Gretchen, and their four daughters. Pronek readily accepted the invitation, although he knew very well that he would never see Simon again.

The hotel was a Quality Inn.

Pronek would remember—to this day—the room at the Quality Inn with eerie clarity: there was a large double bed in a green cape staring at the ceiling with its pillow eyes; a dark TV facing the bed patiently, like a dog waiting for a treat; an ascetic chair, opening its wooden arms in invitation to a bland desk; an umbrellaed lamp, casting its light shyly on the writing surface; a heavy, matronly, peach-colored curtain, behind which there was a large window with a generous vista of an endless wall. The bathroom was immaculately clean, with towels layered upon each other, resembling a snow cube. Pronek kept flushing the scintillating toilet, watching with amazement (he had an entirely different concept of the toilet bowl than we do) how the water at the bottom was enthusiastically slurped in, only to rise, with liquid cocksureness, back to the original level. There were two rubber footprints stuck to the bottom of the bathtub and a handlebar sticking out of the wall. So Pronek cautiously let the water run, stepped onto the rubber footprints, which matched his feet exactly, and grasped the handlebar, but nothing happened.

We cannot be entirely sure what it was that he expected to happen.

He washed his pale-blue underwear and the exhausted collar of his rather unseemly flannel shirt, and then stretched them across the chair. He thrust himself upon the bed, which routinely creaked, and lay naked, trying unsuccessfully to calculate the time difference between Washington and Sarajevo (six hours), until he fell asleep.

He woke up and didn't know where he was or who he was, but then he saw his underwear spreading its pale-blue wings across the chair, providing clear evidence of his existence prior to that moment. He got up, liberated the window from the curtain's oppression, and saw that it was daytime, because some confused light clambered down the wall, and waited outside the window to be let in and scurry to the dark corners. He was delighted with the whole poetic-morning setup, until he found out that his underwear was still moist.

He did not hear the maid because he was drying his pants with a hair dryer, which he discovered in the holster, like a concealed revolver, by the mirror. She boldly walked in and saw him clutching his underwear with his left hand and pressing the hair dryer's muzzle into its face, as if torturing it to confess. We should point out that he was butt-naked and was brandishing a regular morning erection. Pronek and the maid—a slim young woman with a paper tiara on her head—were locked together in a moment of helpless embarrassment, and then Pronek slowly closed the door. He sat on the toilet seat, thinking about the loss of his suitcases, which must have been freezing somewhere up in the heavens, stacked up, with all the other completely foreign and unfamiliar suitcases, in a cavernous underbelly of a plane, heading away, away from him. When he finally put on his broken-down shorts and mustered up enough audacity to face the maid, she was gone. His bed was all straightened up, and there was a piece of red heart-shaped candy on the pillow. Pronek imagined having a passionate affair with the maid, who really was a daughter of a New York billionaire, trying to lead an independent, dignified life and get on with her painting career. He could see himself moving back to New York with her; he would live in a shabby, but homey, apartment in Greenwich Village and support her, making love to her in saxophone slow motion, kissing her graceful hands and dainty cheeks stained with vivid colors.

Simon waited for him at the reception desk, except that he was not Simon, but someone else who looked like Simon, save for the thick glasses and a torus of fat resting on his hips and pelvis. He serenely informed Pronek that he hoped Pronek had slept well, and that Pronek's luggage had been found in Pensacola, Florida. They drove past the same monuments and buildings, in front of which there were insectile machines, plowing away lumps of snow. They (Pronek and Simon no. 2) stopped in front of a large mansion hiding behind a marble-white set of pillars, akin to Gargantuan prison bars. On the lawn, covered with whipped-creamy snow, there was a sign with an eagle spreading its awesome wings, frowning away from the house, as if pissed off at the inhabitants. They walked into a large hall and there was a uniformed guard under a colorful picture of the uncomfortably smirking George Bush.

"Hi, George!" said Pronek's escort.

"Hi, Doc!" said the guard, who stood with his legs spread, and his hands wedged authoritatively in his armpits. Doc disappeared into the office maze behind George's back. George ordered Pronek to wait in the hall, whose walls were covered with paintings of stuck-up men, their cheeks slightly turgid, as if their oral caverns were full of smoke they didn't dare exhale. The same pissed eagle, Pronek noticed, was stretched flatly across the floor, and the ceiling was so high that "the eye struggled in vain to reach the remoter angles," to quote one of our great writers. The sign propped on a scrawny wooden stand said: "No Concealed Weapons." It was cold, so Pronek sat in an armchair, with his hands deep in his pockets, under the gaze of a man with puckered lips and eyebrows in the shape of a distant seagull. Pronek played with marbles, which still lay in transoceanic hiatus at the bottom of his coat pockets, revolving them around each other. Then—to our surprise—a man sped out from behind George's back with his right hand extended in front of him, and a genuinely counterfeit smile. As Pronek was pulling his hand out, he said: "Welcome!" and the marbles, finally freed from lint chains, leapt out of the pocket and began bouncing away from each other, cackling in their sudden liberty. He could still hear the echoes of the runaway marbles from distant corners, when the man asked Pronek: "So, how do you like our capital?"

"I don't know," Pronek said sheepishly. "I just arrived."

"You'll love it!" the man exclaimed. "It's great."

Apocalypse Now

In New Orleans, Pronek stood in line, hoping to buy a real American hot dog, behind a man who had a gigantic black cowboy hat, tight denim pants, and a leather belt pockmarked with silver bolts. As the man walked away biting into his elaborate hot dog, mustard spurting out of the corners of his mouth, the excited vendor kept looking after him: "Whoa, man! Do you know who that is? Do you know who that is? That's Garth Brooks!" The vendor had a baseball hat that was labeled "Saints" and his face had the delicate texture of a ripe pomegranate. "Who is Garth Brooks?" Pronek innocently asked. "Whoa, man! Who is Garth Brooks!? You don't know who Garth Brooks is? Whoa! He's the fuckin' greatest. You gotta be kiddin' me!" Then he addressed (to put it mildly) the next person in line, a young woman in white cowboy boots with little bells on the sides, whose blond hair was all thrust back, as if she had ridden a motorcycle helmetless for a couple of hours. "That's Garth Brooks?" She shrieked and turned to the person behind her—and a chain reaction occurred, which propelled Pronek out of the circle of exultant exclamations. They all looked longingly after Garth Brooks, who was trying to wipe mustard off his black suede boots, but was spreading it all over instead.

Garth Brooks, of course, is one of our finest country musicians.

In Columbus, Ohio, Pronek had dinner at the house of a blue-eyed poet who once won the John Wesley Gluppson Prize, as he was proudly informed by the host's wife. The poet and his wife, both well into their healthy sixties, were kind enough to invite a group of their valued, intellectually distinguished, friends. There was a professor of history, bow-tied, his face frosted with a sagely beard, in a tweed jacket with suede elbow patches, who was an expert on early American history, he said, in particular the Founding Fathers. "Are there Founding Mothers?" Pronek asked whimsically, but was immediately rewarded with a forgiving collective smile. There was a lawyer who once sold a script about injustice, which was never produced, but could have been directed "by Stanley Kramer himself." There was a young mousy woman with droopy eyes who had just come out of a painful, bitter divorce, and was normally a painter deeply interested in Native American spirituality. And let us not forget Pronek, the uncomfortable tourist.

They asked Pronek, who alternately picked at a piece of soy steak and two limpid asparagus corpses, intermittently gulping red Chilean wine, the following questions:

What's the difference between Bosnia and Yugoslavia?

Huge.

Do they have television?

Yes.

Do they have asparagus there?

Yes, but no one in their right mind eats it. (Chortle on the right, chuckle on the left.)

What language do people speak there?

It's complicated.

Is the powder keg going to explode?

Yes.

Is he going to settle in the United States?

Probably not.

Has he ever heard of Stanley Kramer?

Guess Who's Coming to Dinner?

Finally, Pronek toppled over his high wine glass, and then watched in panic, yet catatonic, the red tide spreading westward, toward the woman who had just come out of a painful, bitter divorce. She yelped and said: "Blood! I had a vision of blood last night! Ah!" She pressed her temples and stared at the asparagus corpses heaped in the middle of the table. She kept pressing her temples, as if trying to squeeze her eyes out.

Pronek saw her long black nails bending backward and was afraid that they might break. She began sobbing, and everyone looked at one another, except Pronek, who looked at his supine wine glass. They sat in confounded silence; she wept, her crystal earrings rattling as her head quaked. The John Wesley Gluppson Prize winner then poured a little wine in her glass and said: "There, there now. It's a Chardonnay!" whereupon she looked at him, smiled, and began wiping her tears with the tips of her fingers, whose nails were (to Pronek's relief) unbroken, with the same vigor with which she wept. Pronek said: "I am very sorry."

While in Los Angeles, Pronek met John Milius, because he wrote the script for Pronek's favorite movie, *Apocalypse Now*. His office was in the building that Selznick constructed to stand in for Tara in *Gone With the Wind*—just the front part, in fact, because the building was only one room deep. Besides John Milius, who sat at his vast desk suckling on a cigar as long as a walking stick, there was a man who introduced himself as Reg Buttler. He was abundantly mustached and had on a pale-denim shirt, across whose chest an embroidered line zigzagged, like an EKG-line. He shook Pronek's hand, and, additionally, heartily slapped his shoulder. There was a signed copy of the *Apocalypse Now* script ("From John to Reg") on the table in front of him. Pronek was allotted a large glass of bourbon and a giant cigar.

"Cuban," John Milius said. "The only good thing that communism ever produced." Reg Buttler lit Pronek's cigar, which kept wiggling, too large to handle, between his feeble fingers.

Then Reg Buttler put his right ankle on his left knee, and

pulled the leg violently toward his pelvis, apparently trying to break his own hip. The sharp tip of Reg's elaborately engraved cowboy boot was directly pointed at John Milius, and Pronek thought that if he had a secret weapon in that boot—something that would eject poisonous pellets, for instance—he could kill John Milius in an instant.

"Do you people in Sarajevo like Sam Peckinpah?" Milius asked.

"We do," Pronek said.

"No one made blood so beautiful as the old Sam did," Milius said.

"I know," Pronek said.

"I didn't know you could watch American movies there," Reg Buttler said.

"We could."

"So what's gonna happen there?" Milius asked.

"I don't know," Pronek said.

"Thousands of years of hatred," Reg Buttler said and shook his head compassionately. "I can't understand a damn thing."

Pronek didn't know what to say.

"Hell, I'll call General Schwarzkopf to see what we can do there. Maybe we can go there and kick some ass," Milius said.

"Like we kicked Saddam's ass," said Reg Buttler. "Damn, that was fuckin' good. We kicked that bastard's ass."

"General Schwarzkopf told me," John Milius said, "that the Marines were the best. Those boys are the best."

Pronek inhaled too much cigar smoke, so he abruptly coughed and spurted bourbon on the *Apocalypse Now* script, while a rivulet of snot ran down to his chin.

"War brings out the best and the worst in people," Milius said. "And only the fittest survive."

Pronek took out his hanky and wiped his nose, his chin, and the *Apocalypse Now,* respectively. Reg looked determinedly to the right, then to the left, clearly mulling over a profound thought.

"Do you want to stay in this country?" Milius asked Pronek.

"You should," Reg Buttler said. "It's a damn good country."

"I don't know," Pronek said.

"I'll call General Schwarzkopf and see what we can do about it. Listen, if you have nothing to do tomorrow, we can go out to the shooting range and raise some hell."

"I'm there with ya!" Reg Buttler said.

But Pronek had a meeting that he couldn't miss (which we know was not true) so he politely declined. Before he left, he had a picture taken in front of the building that used to act as Tara. There he is—our foreign friend—teeny with the house in the background, sturdy pillars all lined up behind, like cousins in a family picture, lawns glaring green. He is standing a foot away from Reg and Milius. Milius's hand is resting on Reg's shoulder, the two of them like Scarlett O'Hara and her pop, except there is no fake, painted, blood-red sunset, against which they could appear to be shadows, as the music reaches an orgasmic pitch.

Mud Miracle

Before it began circling like a hawk, waiting to bury its claws into the runway, the plane hit some turbulence, so orange juice leapt out of the trembling plastic cup, looked around and gleefully landed on Pronek's beige pants. Chicago under snow looked like a frosted computer-chip board seen from high above, and—while our foreigner was being lowered—moving vehicles became discernible, little bytes being exchanged between the chips. There was a person with two yellow sticks waving at the plane, as if mesmerizing a dragon. Unbuckling the seat belt, which echoed cavernously all around the plane, Pronek realized that the juice stain had attained the subtle hue of urine.

Andrea was waiting for him at the exit, and as his co-passengers elbowed their way into the molasses of the airport crowd, she offered him her right cheek and her upper body attached to it, while keeping her lower body a couple of feet away, as if a contact between their pelvises would ignite a ferocious intercourse. She told him she was so happy to see him and asked him about his trip. Pronek pointed at the urine-orange stain and joked that his bladder was so small that urine just had to fight its way out, until it could breath freely, the wretched refuse.

Did she laugh? Indeed she did not.

They stood on the moving walkway, gliding through a dark tunnel with sinuous neon lights crawling all over the ceiling, and a synthetic female voice warbling: "Do not leave your baggage unattended!"

Desperate to be charming, Pronek said: "If thing that takes you up is escalator, would this be levelator?"

"Yeah, right," Andrea said.

And now, why not, a quick step back into their common past:

Pronek met Andrea in the summer of '91, in Ukraine. They had a lot of fun, flirting and witnessing the August '91 putsch. They held hands in front of the Ukrainian parliament when it declared independence, while everywhere around them people ruddy with patriotic excitement waved blue-and-yellow flags and demanded freedom and stuff like that. She had a Brit for a boyfriend, who wore a pinkish headband at all times and kept looking for a rave all over Kiev, but never found one. We know that he worked as a cameraman for the BBC, and on the day independence was declared, he was—God bless his hollow heart—very busy. So they walked to the Dnieper and bought a Red Army officer's hat for a couple of dollars, which she wore thereafter. They ate a frisbee-sized pizza, with carrot-and-beets topping. They watched the Dnieper gently flowing, with the scattered, starry glitter of dead-fish bellies. Pronek investigated the inside of her thighs, never getting over the wall of the panty-line, while the tips of their tongues clumsily collided in midair. In a fit of inexplicable giddiness, Pronek susurrously sang a Frank Sinatra song into her ear: "Eye praktis ehvree dai to faind sum klehvr lains to sai, too maik da meenin cum tfruh . . ."

That was one of the songs that his blues band, Blind Jozef Pronek & Dead Souls, well known and liked in Sarajevo, used to play, and, miraculously, she found it endearing.

But the next day she went with her camera-boyfriend to Kharkiv. Pronek went back to Sarajevo and wrote to her a series of, arguably, love letters, full of shades, ochre and auburn, of autumn leaves and reminiscing about the time (the total of some fifty-three hours) they had spent together. She wrote back that she sorely missed him and that she would like to see him again—a desire, Pronek feared, fueled by the unlikelihood of its fulfillment. They fabricated their past days together: in one of her letters they drank sweet wine, whereas in Kiev they had drunk infernal vodka all the time. He remembered her fragrance, although they were both perpetually stinky and sweaty in the city where water pressure was eternally low, so no one knelt under the faucet to wait for moribund droplets. They remembered, with painful intensity, dancing cheek to cheek—in reality (and reality is our business), they idiotically trotted to the rhythm of anachronistic German disco, while hirsute Ukrainian men swarmed around her, repeatedly trying to rub their perspiring bodies against hers. They failed to remember that Pronek could muster no puissance to repel them, while her boyfriend was having a coquettish conversation with the Canadian embassy undersecretary. Having forged a sufficient number of counterfeit memories, she suddenly invited him to Chicago, prompted, perhaps, by a news report about the war in Croatia and "tensions" in Bosnia. It was a gracious invitation—neither of them thought it could ever happen, but then Pronek got the invitation to visit the United States in the capacity of a freedom-loving writer, so he put Chicago in his itinerary.

Therefore, they were happy to be together again.

She looked different when he saw her at the airport: she was paler, her hair was shorter and darker, and she proudly wore a silver nose ring. Nevertheless, he was glad to be going down the highway with her, their car being sluiced with other cars toward the downtown gutter. The skyline looked flat against the blank sky, like the bottom of the Tetris screen, except there were no rectangles coming from above to fill the angular gaps.

Andrea drove through downtown, pointing at humongous, astringent buildings that admitted little light, and announcing their function. It all sounded like oversized gibberish to Pronek: the Board of Trade, the tallest building in the world, the biggest something, the busiest something else. Pronek rolled down the window—the cold pinched their ears instantly—and looked up. He could not see the end of those buildings. "This is how cockroach sees furniture in apartment," Pronek said. "I'm sure," Andrea said.

The few people that walked, bundled, down the streets were trying to retract their heads into their chests. They scuttled toward the warmth of building lobbies, while a chalky mist kept rushing past their shoes, in pursuit of a windless patch of pavement. Andrea and Pronek drove up Lake Shore Drive. Ice floes lingered in the harbor, as if hiding, shivering, from the waves that were clawing at thick layers of dun ice on the piers.

This is a rendition of Pronek's coming to Chicago, in March 1992, on a flight from L.A., with an uncouth stain in his groin area, and love in his heart.

When Andrea unlocked the door (which had a sign saying: "Violators will be towed") of her apartment, a pungent wave of smoke-and-French-fries stench washed off the walls of Pronek's nostrils. "My roommate is a slob," she said, as Pronek (and we with him) panned over the walls specked with ketchup (rather than blood, Pronek decided); a sofa with fluffy stuffing hatching out of its cushions; a stereo and a TV besieged by CDs and videos; a table buried under a wretched army of McDonald's paper bags and cups viciously pierced by slim straws. There were smothered carcasses of cigarette packages and ashtrays brimming with butts and ashes. The window looked, dimly, at a generic brick wall. A porcine black cat ("Her name is Moskva," Andrea said) glanced at Pronek, and then, having found nothing of interest in Pronek's existence, continued staring out the window, at the wall.

Andrea pressed the "play" button on the stereo, and a Madonna song—"Material Girl," we believe—made the cat slither off the sash and run to the kitchen, followed by Andrea and her foreign friend. "I hate fucking Madonna," she said.

"She's a living sexist fantasy. My roommate is a fucking moron." On the kitchen table, there was a mob of beer bottles with their labels ripped off, as if the stout bottles had been tortured and were now awaiting execution. The sink was overflowing with dishes, submerged in murky liquid. Every once in a while, a bubble would reach the surface, eventually bursting with a barely audible belch. There must have been, Pronek thought, a monstrous creature embedded in the sludge at the bottom of the sink.

"Who is your roommate?" Pronek asked.

"He's my boyfriend," Andrea said. "But we have separate bedrooms."

"So, how long you have been together?"

"On and off, about ten years. But I hate the fucker, I think I wanna break up."

"Does he know about me?"

"Oh, yeah. He sure as hell does. I told him you were coming. He doesn't give a fuck. He knows everything."

Well, we happen to know he didn't.

She pushed aside the bottles and they helplessly clinked against each other, until they settled, thick as thieves, on the left side of the table. She pulled two chairs together and put two large cups of coffee at the liberated end of the table, whose surface, Pronek discovered, had prickly tobacco crumbles strewn and stuck to greasy film.

He wanted to touch her apple cheeks, and the shimmering gossamer on the nape of her neck, and the slope of her shoulders, and the little cavern under her breasts, which he had entered but once, in Kiev, and which was, once upon a time, delectably perspirant. He was mesmerized by her lips barely touching each other as she uttered her bs and ms, and her teeth flashed at him as she formed her fricatives. More than anything, it was the way she laughed: leaning slightly to the left and holding her tummy, as if protecting her viscera from spurting out, protruding the tip of her tongue—and finally producing a delightful chortle.

Pronek had fantasized about her, about her "unmediated body"—she did nothing to adorn herself. Her body was an instrument of investigation (this is, mind you, what Pronek thought), not an object to be packaged for men, so she could get them to like her. Pronek was sick of all the Sarajevo men and women who spent time performing little love rituals, designing themselves desirable. He wanted—he believed—true love and a true body with it. Andrea was his Statue of Liberty, a symbol of emotional freedom, a proof of the possibility that two people can *be* (Pronek's italics) for each other, rather than perform love for each other. She could make, he imagined, all those Frank Sinatra songs, all those movies (*Breakfast at Tiffany's, Brigadoon, Gigi*) about the inevitable, unconquerable, transcendental love, she could make that come true.

Hence he carried his two boxy suitcases to her room: her minuscule underwear lounging everywhere; her brassieres hanging, like rabbit skins, from doorknobs; a bag full of shoes and stacks of books on the floor, like a little downtown; the bed with crumpled green covers, kneaded by her body.

That night, they made love.

But before they did, she unrolled a scroll of condoms, and Pronek had to wear one. "This is the nineties," she said. "People can touch each other only if they wear rubber gloves." So he awkwardly put on his one-fingered glove in front of the entertained Andrea. As they were grinding the sheets, and the bed enthusiastically creaked, and the cat, having jumped on the bed, brushed his face with her downy tail, Andrea kept asking: "Isn't this good? Do you like this? Isn't this great?" It was good—the room reeked of bodily fluids and skin friction and dust. They breathed into each other's faces and let their abdomens adhere. Then their little sex unit fissioned, and she went to the bathroom—her silhouette against the kitchen light, Pronek realized, was gorgeous. He disrobed his penis and lay in bed, the condom hanging from his hand, and he thought about his life. We are in a privileged position to assume what his train of thought might have been freighted with: What is going to happen to me? he asked himself. The things back home will never be well. War in Bosnia was likely, if unimaginable. He imagined marrying Andrea and having a writer's career, teaching at a woodsy university. He would wear a tweed jacket with suede patches on the elbows; he would become jug-eared and bespectacled and gray-bearded; he would have season tickets for the symphony; he would frown often, and chuckle at the *New Yorker* cartoons; they would have children who would go to Harvard. He envisioned Andrea and himself, old, yet still in love, their bones shabby, their hair gray, their voices weak, sitting by a fireplace, their backs warm, reading books of the Old Masters, and their lawn would be green and colorful, while carefree warblers would hop all over their modest property. Then a sudden, rapacious itch in his crotch derailed the American-dream train, and Andrea walked in, spreading the scent of a heavenly shampoo. He kissed her wet hair on his way to the bathroom, carrying a dangling condom before him, as if it were a dead rat.

And the moment before he was to step into the bathroom, its doors amicably opened, the steam speedily leaving it, a man walked into the apartment. For reasons inexplicable, Pronek didn't slip into the bathroom ("Come in," whispered the steam), but stood there, nude as a piglet, suddenly aware of the hairlessness of his chicken chest, and general grotesqueness of man's frontal nudity, not to mention the gooey condom in his hand.

"Hi!" Pronek said.

"How're you doin'?" the man said.

"Good."

"Good."

Silence.

"Who are you?" the man asked.

"I am Andrea's friend."

"I guess," he said. "I'm Carwin." He was fashionably unshaven and had unruly hair, which, to us, signified cynical rebelliousness. He wore an unbuttoned flannel shirt and a T-shirt underneath, with a picture of a crucified, blond angel.

"Are you Russian?" he asked.

Pronek's bare feet were cold, so he put his left sole on his right calf, and stood there like a Masai warrior, with a used condom instead of a spear.

"No, I'm from Sarajevo, Bosnia," Pronek said. "But we met in Ukraine."

"Well, it's nice to meet you," he said. "I hope I'll never see your fucking face again." Then he hollered toward Andrea's room: "Now you started bringing in fucking foreigners. American dick is not good enough for you, you fucking bitch!"

"Fuck you, you fucking Anglo asshole!" she yelled back.

It was then that Pronek finally slipped into the bathroom. The condom wouldn't sink in the toilet bowl, so Pronek kept flushing it, but it would always come back up from the toilet throat, defiantly bobbing. A roll of toilet paper hid behind the toilet seat, like a frightened hedgehog. We can attest that Pronek felt profound helplessness at that moment. A jury of plastic bottles, bemused by the ablution he had to perform, was lined up on the shelf: Natural Care, Head & Shoulders, Happy,

Antarctica, Morning Mist, Mud Miracle (Swiss Formula), No
More Tangles. He looked into the mirror and saw vermilion
dots on his face and sallow teeth and a square Slavic head with
a flat pate and a tuber-nose and greasy hair, sticking to his low
forehead. "What am I doing here?" he asked himself (Patience, dear fellow, patience). But there was nothing that could
be done, there was nothing more inevitable than taking a
shower at that moment.

Pennsylvania 1760

Perhaps it is important to know that Andrea was an artist, indeed a painter. She showed Pronek her most recent finished
painting, a couple of years old, picturing her between a hog
and a sow—all three of them stared at Pronek, framed, presumably, by a farm fence. The pigs were adamantly pink. The
hog seemed to enjoy the situation and it had two dun marks on
its front hams, while the sow had swollen teats. The painting
was entitled *Home*. She informed Pronek, who could not decide whether he liked it or not, but said he liked it anyway, that
she hadn't painted anything after that. "There are things I
need to understand about myself before I can share them with
people," she said.

She worked at the Art Institute, in the gift shop. In the
mornings, she would suddenly erect her upper body in bed, the
way maidens in horror movies wake up from torturous nightmares, just before the killer (who is always in the vicinity)
leaps at them to slice them up. Then she would light a cigarette and look worried. Pronek could tell from the way she
smoked that her life was an arduous task: her forehead would
corrugate; she would slide her tongue between her gums and

the inside of her lips, as if answers to all questions were hiding in oral corners along with food bits; she would wedge her elbow into the palm of her left hand, and prompt her right hand with a cigarette, close to her mouth, nibbling on the filter, inhaling in small, intense gasps, and then exhaling with a burdened, low sigh at the end, like a full stop. She would scratch her spine with her left-hand thumb, and her shoulder blades would move toward each other under the taut skin, only to retreat back to their starting positions.

Pronek would hear the delicate scraping of her long nail against the skin, and, still steeped in his nightmare, he would worry about her birthmarks being ripped off her back.

He would watch her stealthily, not making a sound. When she turned toward him, he would pretend to sleep, keeping his eyes and mouth closed, lest she kiss him, for he was ashamed of his putrescent morning breath. She would trudge to the bathroom, and he would hear the relentless hum of the shower, intermingled with splashing, as if she were resisting a deluge. Then the hair dryer buzz, after which, he suspected, she took care of her hair and her armpits and her lips. By the time she would come back to their room (albeit Pronek would have never referred to it as "our room") he was asleep, and not even the bustle of her picking through her wardrobe, and the rustle of her rolling stockings up her legs would make him open his eyes.

He would get up a couple of hours later and then follow her scent to the bathroom, where she would still be vaporously present, and the bathtub would still have the unfortunate vestiges of her hair, curled up here and there, waiting to be collected in the mass grave of the drain. Pronek would perform his morning toilet duties, trying to make his body presentable to America. There were three toothbrushes, two of which—Pronek's and

Andrea's—lay side by side, as if sunbathing together, while the third one was, incidentally, on the verge of the sink.

It was the third one that Pronek dipped in the toilet water.

On some mornings, Pronek would salvage a plate, not yet engendering mold patches, from the dish-swamp, and eat some limp cheese (invariably mozzarella) and rancid crackers. Sometimes he would sip coffee from a cup that had lipstick scars on the opposite side of the brim, and kept staring at a blank page, only to write "Chicago, April 1992" in the upper-right-hand corner and then stare again, until he would finally abort the letter. He could never go beyond the place and the date, as if those were perfectly self-explanatory, and nothing else need have been said. He wanted to call his parents, but had no money to pay for it, and Andrea had said that he should ask Carwin, since he was "the phone man of the house." Sometimes he would watch the news, showing barricades, and people running in panic, and white, innocent, armored vehicles parked in the middle of a Sarajevo street.

On the days he didn't go to work as a Pier 1 store manager, Carwin would get up and lodge himself on the sofa, stick his hand into his flannel shorts, and watch the news with our foreigner. He would say: "Man, I don't understand this shit. Can't they just chill out, man. I mean, what's the big fucking deal?" Pronek would say nothing, stroking the purring Moskva, and then he would get on the downtown train to meet Andrea for lunch.

He would walk down the Magnificent Mile, sweating in his dark coat, dotted with lint, reeking of traveling and the past. Often, he would be thinking about *The Magnificent Seven* and *Seven Samurai* and there was nothing magnificent about the mile: morgue-like buildings and lugubrious stores promis-

ing all kinds of purchasable joys. Whenever he found himself
walking down the Magnificent Mile, he had a burning craving
for a McDonald's burger, which he normally hated and considered inedible, respectively.

Perhaps this could be Pronek's contribution to the psychol-
ogy of architecture.

He would stroll past people clutching their purses or briefcases, frowning at the wind. "Who are they?" he wondered.
"Where do they live? What do they do?" Once he realized,
schlepping through the goo and yuck of wet April snow, that
he was utterly superfluous walking down the Magnificent
Mile, that everything would be exactly the same if the space
his body occupied at that moment were empty—people would
walk with the same habitual resolve, clutching the same
purses and briefcases, perhaps even infinitesimally happier, because there would be more walking space without his body.
When he shared his thoughts with Andrea, she said, with a
nasty giggle: "The land of the free, the home of the brave."

Pronek would wait for Andrea to get her lunch break, and
he would roam the shop, browsing through postcards, trying
on aprons adorned with Picasso or Monet pictures, reading
books on African art. Once he located all the cameras in the
store, disinterested little eyes gazing from distant upper corners, and tried to find a spot not covered by a camera, and
found none. Sometimes he would just find an inconspicuous
position in the store, hiding behind a curtain of posters, or pre-
tending to be reading a book, and he would watch Andrea
smiling at the customers, gracefully returning their credit
cards, or handing a bagful of artful merchandise over the
counter. Then she would get off and they would drift through
the museum, never holding hands. They would hide in the
American Furniture and Arts section, where they would ven-

ture into illicit, deliciously dangerous, touching, under the
worried, worried gaze of George Washington; or under the
conjugal gaze of Mr. and Mrs. Daniel Hubbard—Daniel's
promontory chin reaching into the glorious revolutionary future; or the sovereignly chaste gaze of Abigail Cheseborough.
Of course, most of these names meant nothing to Pronek, but
they all looked devoutly uncomfortable. Pronek and Andrea
would pussyfoot around a Lincoln staring at marble tiles under
their feet, apparently pensive, in duck-beak boots and with a
duck-beak beard, stepping forward, his hands locked on his
leaderly butt. And there was a Lincoln welded to an uncomfortable brazen chair, worried all over again, wearing the same
boots, except Pronek could see the big-toe lumps and imagine
the sweaty, swollen feet and the ingrown toenails causing a lot
of banal pain.

They would roam through the armor section, where metal
man-sheaths suggested an eerie presence, as if the bodies that
were meant to fill those armors were stored somewhere in the
warehouse. They would follow a battalion of high school kids,
predominantly blond and obese ("Cornfed," Andrea would
whisper), who were hee-hawing in front of naked-lady paintings, as their faces worked on the spring collection of pimples.
They would start looking at paintings of the fourteenth century, and then move chronologically, with everyone else, counterclockwise. It seemed to Pronek that between the fourteenth
and seventeenth centuries the main human activities were suffering, torture, fear, and rape. "Did you have the sixteenth century in Sarajevo?" Andrea asked him once. "Yeah," our friend
said. "But it was different." He would try to sound cultured
and civilized—to play the role of a European, as it were—and
make the most of his two-hour visit to the Louvre, which he
had mainly spent lost in a nightmarish eighteenth-century

wing. He would try to devote a reasonable portion of thinking to each painting, but would often find himself staring at the carved frames and blank walls around the painting, yawning like an excited monkey. In the room that contained some *Rape of Lucrece* he stared at Lucrece's torn pearl necklace eternally in midair and thought about the incredible amount of yawning that could be witnessed in museums, mainly because of the lack of air circulation, as if breathing would impair understanding of Great Art.

A senior citizen in a glaring pink jacket stopped in front of the *Rape* and gasped.

Her favorite painting was humongous and completely black—black wrinkles, black smudges, black puckered paint, and Pronek liked it, but didn't know why. They would gawk at it for a while and Andrea would say: "Who are we in the hands of an angry God?"

One day, Pronek and Andrea descended to the miniature rooms. "Begin to your left," said the sign on the wall, and when they began to their right, an elderly lady, the Cerberus of the miniature rooms, with a puffy hairdo and thin lips, issued a warning with a fiery glance and a significant tightening of her lips, so they began to their left. There was a fair-haired brat darting around like a crazed colt, and occasionally peering behind the pane into the miniature rooms. Then he would start running around again and holler: "Awesome, baby! Awesome, baby!" The rooms were small, very small. Pronek had never seen anything like that. A "Pennsylvania 1760" room had minuscule armchairs and desks, and a minute fireplace, with tiny fake flames. There was a little carpet and wee windows, and, behind them, a garden illuminated by an invisible sun. Pronek was the only one looking into the "Pennsylvania 1760" room, so he was the only one to see a minikin figure, with long white hair, and an impish mini-grin, running across the miniature room. Pronek could hear the tapping, the barely audible, evanescent, echoes of the creature's tiny steps, which then disappeared into the garden.

Doubtless, a hallucination.

The brat was revolving around a center invisible to anyone but him, still shrieking; "Awesome, baby!" but then he got much too dizzy and collapsed on the floor. He lay right below a "Virginia 1790" room, holding his blond watermelon in his hands, panting, still saying: "Awesome, baby!"

Andrea went with Pronek to check out his coat, and Pronek said: "How can you ever know that you're getting right coat? Maybe everything you have is replaced by something else. I think, maybe they're going through your pockets. They're photographing what's in there, making keys, and changing everything. So when you get out, everything is different, and your memories don't look right, so you change them." He put his coat on. "You know what I mean? I cannot ever know that this is my real, old coat, but I must wear it anyway, because there's no other coat, and I must make memories about it."

"You Eastern Europeans are pretty weird," Andrea said.

When Pronek came back home (albeit it was Andrea's home), Carwin leapt off the couch, in all likelihood interrupted while masturbating, and hurried to his room. Pronek changed the channel from *The Dukes of Hazzard* to CNN and saw a crowd of people in front of the parliament building in Sarajevo, cowering and hastening to find cover, or just roaming, confused by the sniper fire. There was a quick shot of a sneakered foot paired with a sneakerless foot, both twitching, and a rotund big toe protruding, while the rest of the body was obscured by a cluster of people trying to help, some of them crying and wiping their tears with bloody hands.

Then there was the national weather forecast, so Pronek got up and got himself a dirty glass of ginger ale.

The Question of Bruno

Jozef Pronek decided to stay in the United States, possibly for the rest of his life, in the middle of a snowy night, as snowflakes were pressing their crystal faces against the window pane, after Carwin dropped a pot of rotting spaghetti on the floor and said: "Fuck!" He woke up, his heart pounding again (yes, it had pounded before), having dreamt of dogs tearing his body apart—a German shepherd going for his throat, a poodle for his calves. Through the door ajar, he could see Carwin trying to clean and spreading the red mush, as if painting, all over the floor. It looked like blood and brains to Pronek. He imagined himself lying on that floor, the insides of his head slowly leaking out, feeling no pain, just dizziness. Carwin, having pensively scratched his crotch, decided to abandon the cover-up, said: "Fuck!" once again to seal his uncompromising decision, and then stomped toward the couch to watch TV.

Next morning he woke up ill, with his forehead and the nape of his neck throbbing. Andrea was gone, he heard the TV, but he couldn't get up, so he closed his eyes and plummeted to the bottom of slumber. He kept coming in and out of listless dreams about Sarajevo, in which (for example) he would try to draw the map of the city in English, but couldn't do it, because he couldn't draw in English. Or he would be walking down his street (passersby carrying pointed black umbrellas, looking at

him askance) and it would impossibly intersect with the wrong
street, so he couldn't find the right direction.

The banal symbolism of these dreams notwithstanding, we
should note that they suggest the situation of being in a maze.

Andrea came back home after work, made some tea for
Pronek, gave him a bowl of Wheaties floating in glistening
milk, kissed his cold forehead (in between surges of fever) and
then took off to a gallery opening. She didn't come back that
night, and Pronek kept sweating, until the sheets were so
soaked, sticking to his febrile body, that he had to get up and
rummage through her closets, looking for virgin sheets, only to
find a notebook with a little lock, under a pyramid of towels.
But Pronek was shivering and had no strength to read it, fearing that he might find out things he didn't care to know. So he
took a couple of towels and spread them, like magic carpets, on
the naked mattress, and proceeded to perspire. He didn't know
how long he stayed in bed—intermittent kisses, tepid cups of
tea, and waking up in a cold, moist bed all merged into one
long repetitive action, like a busy signal. If we were to ask him
now, he could probably remember the wind banging at the
window, and infernal electronic voices shrieking "Touchdown!
Hee hee hee . . . !" He would have a dim recollection of calling
his parents: his father told him it would be unwise to come
back to Sarajevo, while his mother told him that there already
was less shooting than yesterday, and that they missed him.

Once he mustered up some energy, while the fever was
recovering somewhere in his body, and found Carwin and a
legion of his buddies gathered around the TV, which had a
porn flick on. It took Pronek a while to recognize the gaping
vagina—the slurping sound it was making confused him. But
they weren't watching it, they were deeply invested in throwing a hacky sack at the revolving ceiling fan, which would

slam the hacky sack against the wall every now and then. In celebration of the fan's success, someone would say, "Shit!" and get to suck on the pot pipe, shaped as the Grim Reaper.

There was a guy named Chad, and he was a history student.

Chad stayed for the rest of the week, sleeping on the couch, because he had to play a season of Tecmo Bowl with Carwin: Carwin was the Cowboys, while Chad was the Redskins. Pronek spent that week between the bed and the kitchen table, sometimes trying to write letters, but all of his sentences would fall apart before reaching the paper. Andrea had disappeared. Carwin claimed that she went to DeKalb for a couple of weeks, because she needed a break. Occasionally, between virtual football games and porn flicks, Pronek got to watch *Headline News* and learn that paramilitary ("Pornomilitary" punned Chad) units were entering Bosnia from Serbia. Carwin and Chad watched images of men in fatigues and a woman talking about massacres of Muslims in the eastern parts of Bosnia.

"This is depressing," Carwin said.

"What's with you people," Chad asked. "Can't you chill out?"

"They just hate each other over there," Carwin said.

"Are you going back?" Chad asked.

"I'm supposed to fly back in couple of weeks," Pronek said.

"Why don't you stay here?" Chad asked.

"What can I do?" Pronek said. "My family is there."

"Man, I wish I'd never see my fuckin' family again," Carwin said and wedged his hand furiously into his pants.

"You should stay and get your family out and let those fuckers kill each other if they want," Chad said. Chad had an uncanny ability to bend his legs so much that he would effortlessly sit in the lotus position, like an Indian sage, while playing football, his thumbs pressing the buttons with incredible speed.

"I mean, fuck, war is good. If we didn't have war, there would be way too many people, man. It's like natural selection, like the free market. The best get on the top, the shit sinks. I don't know much about you, Russkie, and I don't like you, but if you got here you must be worth something. It's like those immigrants, man, they were shit at home, they got here, they became fucking millionaires. That's why we're the toughest motherfucking country in the world. Because only the fittest survive here."

Carwin was sucking on a McDonald's straw, watching the news about the Bulls. "Man," he said. "We're gonna kick ass this year again." Pronek crawled back into his (well, Andrea's) room and lay there, while the dusk was setting in, until he could see twig shadows trembling on the wall.

Andrea came back from DeKalb the next morning, refreshed. "Boy," she said. "I was tripping for days." When she entered the room, Pronek was heading to the bathroom to look in the mirror, stepping over the red pasta-sauce sea on the floor. He had two weeks' worth of minuscule growth on his face, which made his face look smudged with coal dust, and he was wearing her bathrobe, his shorts barely hanging on to his hips.

He had lived on Carwin's supply of Twinkies for two weeks.

That morning he woke up after a night of unsettling dreams, and saw his body as someone else's body. His toes were miles away; his knees were two round dunes. He looked at his hands and they raised their heads to look back at him with hostility. He didn't know what he was. But when Andrea walked in and looked at him, he suddenly recognized himself as a foreigner—uncouth, unseemly, unpleasant body, with nowhere to go. He went to the bathroom, and shaved and washed, performing a ritual, as if celebrating his new identity.

Next day, they went to Andrea's parents' house for dinner.

They drove down Lake Shore Drive, the waves attacking the shore, while trees bent sideways, as if stretching their backs in an aerobic exercise. Andrea whistled and wheezed "Dear Prudence," and after they listened to the newsbreak that talked about the imminent war in Bosnia, she said: "You should stay, you know." "I know," Pronek said. The street lights had glaring clarity, because of the frigid northern wind. They drove past the dark castles of the University of Chicago ("This is where they built the first nuke bomb," she said) and entered a maze of identical red-brick buildings.

Andrea's father vigorously shook Pronek's hand and her mother said: "We've heard so much about you." Then they presented him to an old woman, bent over a walker, holding its handles passionately, as if she were delivering a speech from a pulpit. "Nana," Andrea's mother said. "This is Andrea's friend from Bosnia."

"I never was in Boston," Nana said.

"Bosnia, Nana, Bosnia. In Yugoslavia, near Czechoslovakia," Andrea's mother said, shook her head, and waved her hand as if pushing away a basketball, asking Pronek to forgive Nana. In a moment of confusion, Pronek took off his shoes. Andrea's mother glanced at his feet, then locked her hand, pointing to the left, in front of her bosom and said: "Let's move to the salon."

They sat at a round table, under an illustrious lantern, with heavy pieces of crystal pending above their heads. Andrea's father filled their glasses with wine. He stood over Pronek with the lean greenish bottle in his hand, waiting for him to try the wine. Pronek sipped, and the glass chinked against his teeth, but then he said: "It's good. Little sweet."

"Well, it's a Chardonnay," Andrea's father said, delighted.

Nana sat across the table from Pronek, smacking her lips and wiggling her jaw, and they could all hear the dentures steadily clacking. Her face looked like a map—valleys, furrows, wrinkles, cheekbones protruding like mountains. "I want wine," she said. "Where's my wine?" She kept moving her mouth, as if chewing the unchewable.

"It's not good for you, Nana," Andrea's mother said. "You know that."

"What kind of wine do you have back home?" Andrea's father asked, slanting his head to the left to signal intense interest.

"I don't know," Pronek said. "Local kinds."

"Hmm," Andrea's father said.

"Andrea told us you were a writer," Andrea's mother said. She had fenestral glasses, and a pearl choker, and her teeth were white and orderly, like an ivory keyboard. Andrea's father wore a tweed jacket with elbow patches, his ears were flappy, and when he stood against the light, Pronek could see a pink penumbra around his earlobes.

"I was," Pronek said.

"We like good writing," Andrea's mother said.

"Have you ever read Richard Ford?" Andrea's father asked.

"Sensitive middle-class macho shit," Andrea snapped and looked at Pronek, who simply said: "No."

"Very well written," Andrea's father said and shook his head, as if rattling it. "Very well written."

"And we like Kundera," Andrea's mother said. "He's from Czechoslovakia, too."

"Who's in the kitchen?" Nana asked, pricking up her ears,

burdened by grayish clusters. She had twiggish arms from which crumpled skin hung like drying dough. She had a dim number tattooed between two veins on her right forearm.

"No one's in the kitchen, Nana. We're all here," Andrea's father said and googled his eyes at Pronek, asking for solidarity.

Andrea's mother served a sequence of foods unknown to Pronek, with the taste and texture of minced cardboard ("This is wild rice," she beamed at him nacreously), which he ate carefully, fearing a sudden accident, like chewing with his mouth open, or dropping a forkful of wild rice and salad "with maple-syrup-and-sunflower-seed dressing" into his lap. Pronek had a penetrating sense that his feet were about to begin exuding stench, so he covered his left-foot toes with his right foot, but then fretted that the hissing of sock friction might become too loud. He was convinced that he should move as little as possible, lest unnecessary motion release mischievous molecules of bodily odor.

"Who's not here?" Nana asked. She would load her mouth and then chew patiently, looking at them with weary disinterest. Her hair was platinum white, but pink patches were clearly visible under the fluff, and her skull was right under the skin, it was right there, Pronek thought.

Then they had blackberry nonfat cheese cake with low-fat kiwi frozen yogurt and French hazelnut vanilla decaf coffee.

"So what's going on in Czechoslovakia," Andrea's mother asked.

"Yugoslavia, Mom, Yugoslavia," Andrea said.

"I read about it, I tried to understand it, but I simply can't," Andrea's father said. "Thousands of years of hatred, I guess."

"It's a sad saga," Andrea's mother said. "It's hard for us to understand, because we're so safe here."

"It's mind-boggling," Andrea's father said.

"Where is Bruno? Is Bruno there in kitchen?" Nana hollered all of a sudden. "Bruno, come here."

"Calm down, Nana. That's not Bruno. Bruno's gone," Andrea's mother said.

"Come here, Bruno!" Nana yelled toward the kitchen. "Eat with us! We have everything now!"

"Calm down, Nana. Or you'll have to go to your room," Andrea's father said and turned to Pronek. "She can be rather obstreperous sometimes." Pronek didn't know what "obstreperous" meant, so he just said: "It's okay. No problem." Nana jiggled her jaw and calmed down. Andrea's mother was scraping off the remnants of food, little piles of mush, onto a big plate.

"What you will do with it?" asked Nana. "Don't throw it away, Bruno is hungry. Bruno!"

"We're not going to throw it away," Andrea's mother said. "We'll save it for Bruno." Nana's dentures clattered, rejoicing. She had a quick slurp of coffee and then looked at Pronek.

"Who are you?" she asked.

"I'm Andrea's friend," Pronek said.

"Good," she said.

While Pronek was putting on his shoes, revealing the dirt at their prows, Andrea's father was holding his coat. "You should dry clean it," he said. "I know," Pronek said. Andrea's mother pressed her cheek, soft and redolent of coconut, against Pronek's, and kissed the air around his ear. "It was nice having you," Andrea's father said, shaking Pronek's hand with habitual vigor. "I'm sure you'll do fine if you stay here. This is the greatest country in the world, you just have to work hard."

"That's true," Andrea's mother said.

"Are you going to see Bruno?" Nana asked.

"No, Nana," Pronek said. "I'm sorry."

Romaine Lettuce,
Iceberg Lettuce

Pronek got up, put on his best clothes: a gray silk shirt, once
upon a time smuggled from China by a family friend, with an
amoeba-shaped grease blot in the left-nipple area, as if involuntary lactation had taken place; the well-known orange-
stained beige pants; a tie with a Mickey Mouse pattern, lent
and consequently tied by Carwin; a peach-colored jacket, also
generously lent by Carwin, who hadn't worn it for years, one
size too small, hence rather tight in the shoulders, so Pronek,
with his arms protruding, looked like a sad forklift. He put on
his shoes, which had tufts of algae-like dirty lint, once upon a
time fake fur, sticking out on the sides.

This is the attire in which Pronek entered the American
labor market.

Pronek let Moskva out, then followed her down the stairs.
He thought of dust speckles whirling in the sunbeams as puny
angels, although they paid little attention to him. He stood behind the screen door, as if waiting for a cue to enter the stage,
looking down the street: tree-crowns were all upset, swaying
furiously; the wind was flipping their leaves, as if to show they
were unmarked. A man with a rottweiler that looked like the
man's canine self—the same pelican chin, the same doleful
trot—bagged a handful of shit and then carried it reverently
like a piece of valuable evidence, following the investigative,
sniffing dog. The two alcoholic sisters, with identical plum eye
bags, were heading toward their morning refreshment, bicker-
ing about who was culpable for not replenishing the booze sup-
plies, still holding hands. There was a white Cadillac jalopy

parked on the street, with the sign in the windshield saying: "Don't tow it's mine," signed by "Jose." The sky grumbled, as if someone were moving furniture in the universe above. He looked at the sky's underbelly, at the clouds pressing the anxious trees, and enthusiastically frowned—it would rain again, he reckoned. He walked down Norwood, turned north on Broadway, facing the advancing traffic. He waited to cross Broadway at Granville—DON'T WALK the street light warned him. He imagined trying to run across the street and stumbling, a yellow cab trying to avoid his fallen body, but managing to run its front left wheel over his head, crushing it. He imagined the last thing he would see: the greasy underside of a car, layers of dirt covering the axle. He looked in our direction (although we are everywhere) before—WALK—crossing, and proceeded toward the El.

But then he saw a sign in the misty window of the ice cream parlor saying COME IN, so he decided to have some ice cream. He greeted the owner (in English), a Russian man who grew his mustache in proportion to the growth of his business.

At this particular moment, it was the thin mustache of a passionate toreador.

Pronek got a large scoop of rainbow sorbet, and began licking it with ardor immediately, careful to devote equal attention to each color, his tongue becoming multicolored in the process. He foolishly glanced at the corner drug dealer, who mad-dogged him for an intense moment. Pronek collected himself enough to look down at the tips of his shoes, which were habitually uncomfortable, while his tormented big toe occasionally wiggled in pain.

As the train was stopping, he licked away the rainbow and munched away the cone. A sliding door opened right before him ("Open Sesame," he thought). He entered the car and the door closed behind him. "Twenty-two minutes to downtown," said a sign. The car was empty, except for the man who talked to his hands. Pronek had seen him before: the man gibbering into his palms, his hands supine in his lap, every now and then poking the center of his left palm with his right index finger, pressing a magic button. The clatter and murmur of the speeding train made Pronek drowsy, so he closed his eyes. He heard the hum of his blood, and for reasons not known to us, a rather meaningless sequence of words reached the spawny surface of his mind: "Split my head like a watermelon." He opened his eyes and saw the new passengers, just materialized around him, inconspicuously surrounding him. The man who talked to his palms was collecting every piece of paper he could find: he would slide under the seats to retrieve a leaflet saying: "Lord is with you"; he would empty McDonald's bags on the floor, and then fold them up; he would stuff newspaper pages into his trench coat, covered with different shades of filth. Finally, he sat in front of Pronek and began peeling off a Guardian Angels sticker on the window, as if his job were to collect evidence of a vast crime. The man kept refrowning, waves of worries slamming against the inside of his forehead. Pronek watched his long yellow nails with a crescent of gray dirt clawing the sticker, then he panned to the man's temple and saw (zoom) a louse crawling through the man's ashen hair.

Split my head like a watermelon.

Downtown Chicago had streets named after deceased presidents, and Pronek thought that it was built as the presidents played monopoly in heaven (or hell, let us not be presumptuous), and then piled up buildings on their streets after a favorable roll of the dice. Pronek went eastward down Jackson to Michigan Avenue, and then walked north, until he found the Boudin French Sourdough Bakery.

A woman, labeled Dawn Wyman by a little steel name tag on her semitransparent shirt, was waiting for him. Her hair was puffed up, as if there was a steady stream of warm air coming out of her skull. Her eyelids were efficiently blue, echoing the hue of her skirt. She had eyeball-shaped earrings, whose quaking pupils glared at Pronek.

"Where are you from?" Dawn asked.

"Bosnia," Pronek said.

"That's in Russia, right?"

"It was in Yugoslavia."

"Right. Well, tell me why you would like to work for us."

A man with a white cowboy hat was sitting in the corner, under a picture of the first Boudin Bakery, established in San Francisco in the black-and-white times. He was excavating shit-brown spoonfuls of something from a round loaf of bread. Then he determinedly shoved the plastic spoon into his mouth.

"I like European touch here," Pronek said.

"Right," Dawn said and routinely smiled. There was a shade of lipstick on her white teeth. "We like to provide something different, something for the customer with sophisticated taste and international experience."

"Right," Pronek said.

"What do you think you can offer to the Boudin French Sourdough Bakery?"

The man in the cowboy hat dropped the spoon in the loaf, smacked his lips, then took off his big hat and wiped his melon, with a bulbous wart above the right eyebrow. He put his hat back on, stood up, pulled his pants to the middle of his belly, then emptied the tray into a garbage bin. The loaf slid into the black gaping orifice of the bin, and Pronek heard the whump.

"I can offer hard work and life experience. I am hard worker and I like to work with people. I used to be journalist and communicated very much," he said.

"Right," Dawn said, looking at the application, uninterested. "What do you expect your wage to be?"

"I don't know. Ten dollars for hour."

"We can offer you five, and maybe later you can work your way up. Here everyone has a fair chance."

"Good," Pronek said.

Thus Pronek became a member of the large Boudin French Sourdough family, and was consequently given the respectable and responsible duty of kitchen help.

He cut croissants open, spread Dijon mustard all over their insides ("Not too much," Dawn would suggest in passing), and then pass them on to the sandwich person ("This is the sandwich person. This is the kitchen help," Dawn introduced them to each other). He was taken off that job, after he nearly sliced off his left thumb and passed on a sequence of blood-soaked croissants to the sandwich person. He would cut tomatoes into thin slices ("Thinner," Dawn would suggest in passing), and he would sprinkle cheese crumbles over a platoon of mini-pizzas. He would fill up styrofoam bowls with the reduced-sodium, fat-free Cajun gumbo soup, and pass them on to the soup person, until he dipped his incised thumb into a scorching jumbo gumbo ("Small bowl—large gumbo. Big bowl—jumbo gumbo," Dawn succinctly explained the essence of the gumbo situation), whereupon he dropped the bowl on the floor, earning a couple of burns on his ankles. He would cut off the top of a sourdough loaf, and then disembowel it, throwing the soft yeast-smelling viscera into a garbage can, feeling dreadfully guilty for some reason, so he ate a lot of it the first day, and received gut-wrenching cramps as a punishment. Then he would fill up the hollow with reduced-fat chili.

The first time he went to the safe-like Frigidaire to get a lettuce head, the doors closed slowly behind him and he found himself in the midst of an immutable gelid hum, feebly lit by a solitary bulb. He imagined freezing to death, being found frosted, his eyes wide open, minuscule icicles on his eyelashes, lying with his pate stuck in a crate of lettuce. He began pounding the door, yelping for help, but no one was out there, no one could hear him. He leaned his head against the door in moribund desperation, and his forehead stuck to the icy surface. He tried to peel it off, but it was painful and he was overwhelmed by fatalistic weakness.

So when Dawn opened the door, he stumbled out, his forehead pulled by the force of Dawn, and then stood before her with a scarlet mark across his forehead.

"What are you doing?" she asked, her plucked eyebrows rising into two symmetrical nail clips.

"I was closed there," Pronek said.

"You can open the door from the inside, you just have to push it a little," she said.

"Oh, I know," Pronek said and hastened toward the safety of dish-washing duties.

From that point on in his food-service career, Pronek was firmly in charge of garbage disposal. He became an apprentice to a man named Hemon. Pronek didn't know whether Hemon was the man's first or the man's last name, but he was from the Dominican Republic, and came to the United States to become a professional soccer player. Pronek inferred Hemon's soccer dream, after he pointed at himself and kept repeating: "Mc-Mannaman," and then made the motion of kicking a soccer

ball. Hemon was tall and, Pronek thought, not particularly intelligent, although he would say nothing, since he spoke no
English. They would empty abandoned trays with hollowed-
out loaves, mauled croissants, desiccated bowls, into garbage
bins; they would pull out loaded garbage bags, tie a knot
around the bag's throat and drag them like corpses ("Hurry,"
Dawn would suggest in passing) to the garbage cart in a back
nook of the kitchen. Pronek would push the cart with Hemon,
who did it with habitual despondency, down the hall beyond
the kitchen, through the mean swinging doors that would always slam their backs or heels, then wait for the elevator.
There was a little camera above the door, glaring down at
them. They would stare at the elevator door in silence, waiting
for it to slide open. They would press the lowest button and
stand by the garbage, separated by the cart, as if they were
honorary guards saluting an important casket. They would go
all the way to the bottom, sinking into the molasses of silence,
and when the door would slide open, a billow of cold, putrescent air would slap their faces. They would push the cart into
a low-ceilinged grotto with a humongous garbage container,
often brimming over with the black garbage bags, in its center.

To their simple minds, this was the supreme garbage bin,
to which they were compelled to offer daily oblations.

They would push the cart onto an altar-like lift, hook up
the axle of the cart, then raise it to the edge of the container.
One of them would push a red button that would make the
altar flip over and empty out the cart. Often, the cart would
just maliciously drop in, and they would have to enter the
supreme garbage bin, which would groan with pleasure. They
would have to lift the cart above their heads, up to their knees
in rotting food, and midwife it out of the bin, as a mixture of
mayo, Dijon mustard, vinegar, gumbo, and reduced-fat chili

crawled down their forearms. They would wash the garbage remnants out of the cart, wash their hands ("Employees must wash their hands," the sign over the sink said) never being able to wash thin lines of dirt out of the furrows of their palms.

At their lunch breaks, Pronek and Hemon would sit in bilingual silence, gawking at the people occupying Boudin tables: a man with a dragon spewing fire on his forearm and a patch over his eye, slurping jumbo gumbo, meticulously unshaven; a lone, slender, black woman reading *Seven Spiritual Laws of Growth*, having bitten off only the tip of her crescent croissant; an obese four-member family, with the same pumpkin heads, round girths and oblong calves, as if they belonged to a species that reproduced by fission; a gentleman in a austere navy-blue suit, with standard CEO gray hair and rimless glasses, reading a surfing magazine, while several leaves of romaine lettuce lay neatly stacked next to his styrofoam plate; two teenage boys sporting facial cobwebs and "Smashing Pumpkins" T-shirts, walled off by a parapet of shopping bags, rating breasts (referring to them as "doves") available in the Boudin French Sourdough Bakery; a bespectacled, perspiring, bald, scrawny man talking to a virgin bag of potato chips ("Do you think I'm afraid of you? Well, you're wrong!"), which Pronek afterward quickly and warily dumped into a bin.

"What kind of evolutional soup did these people's lives emerge from?" Pronek wondered (not in quite so many words and in his native language). "How did they become who they are and not someone else?" He would (wrongly) assume that Hemon might understand him, because of the labor experience they had shared, and he would try to talk to him about the tortuous questions of the randomness of life and death, about how easy it was to become someone else, a complete stranger to oneself, once one lost control of "the river of life."

But Hemon did not understand a word of Pronek's pondering—he would just wearily smile, point at himself with his thumb bent backward and say: "McMannaman!"

Pronek would ride the El back to his (well, Andrea's) place, standing, with the pain in his legs as solid as steel rods, the car full of exhausted people, exuding sweaty fragrances, bunched together, like asparagus in the supermarket.

Andrea went to Ukraine ("I need some space," she said to Pronek. "But you can stay here"), and the apartment was being renovated, since Andrea's parents wanted to sell it. Carwin moved in with Chad, so there were only four Polish construction workers waiting for Pronek, stripping off walls, ripping out door posts, and digging up the floor tiles. There was a nylon path leading to Andrea's room, weighed down with paint cans. Pronek had to go under the ladder, which kept changing its position every day, and then stumbled through the jungle of wet brushes, obscure tools, strewn crooked nails, and paint smudges to get to the room, which now looked like a monk's cell: only the bed, a little tower of books, hollow suitcases, a TV, and a mound of filthy, moist clothes decaying in the corner. He would enter it as if it were a submarine that would take him to the placidity of the ocean bottom: nameless fish, flattened by the incomprehensible pressure of the great water, glimmering plankton and evanescent protozoa floating slowly by his window in absolute, mesmerizing silence. He would stay in the room until the workers were gone and then, disregarding the skinned walls and distended door cavities, he would heat up a can of tomato soup, sprinkle it with some oregano redolent of hay. The sink was empty now, all the plates and mold were gone, except for a single fork, which he used to empty a can of soggy tuna. He would slurp the soup in Andrea's bed, the tuna waiting its turn, watching *Headline*

News: Sarajevo was besieged, there was a severe lack of food, there were rumors of Serbian concentration camps, but he only watched the images to recognize the people in them. Once he thought he saw his father, running down Sniper's Alley, but he couldn't be sure, because the man hid his head behind a folded-up newspaper. The man's gait looked familiar though: big strides, the man slightly bent forward, his right arm swaying like a pendulum.

He would then go to sleep. He stopped turning the light off after he had seen footage of Sarajevo at night, in complete, endless darkness, with bullets and rockets incising and illuminating the sky. His sleep would be well short of restful, marred by nightmares and an anxious bladder.

In the morning, the Polish workers would wake him up with their diligent chitter-chatter. When they began taking the ceiling down they exposed the rib-like beams, and Pronek would have a feeling of waking up inside a whale. The Poles would try to communicate with him, but he couldn't understand them—even though all the words and sounds were disturbingly familiar, as if he were coming back, and very slowly at that, from an abyss of amnesia. He would sit in the kitchen sipping feculent coffee and gnawing on a sapless Twinkie, watching them busting the ceiling, dust coating their bushy eyebrows and basketball-shaped bellies. They held the hammers in their sturdy hands with wide thumbs and flat, broad nails, slamming the ceiling above them with ease.

Pronek imagined those hammers splitting his head like a watermelon.

Pronek got fired the day he saw a picture, framed with the red edges of the *Time* magazine front page, of a man in a Serbian concentration camp: the man stood behind three thin lines of barbed wire, skin tautly stretched across his rib cage, facial hair eating his face away. He was not looking at the camera and the reader behind it, Pronek thought, not knowing whether being in the picture would save him or kill him.

Pronek mumbled his way through the Boudin French Sourdough Bakery kitchen, to his locker, while a surge of heat kept pushing his eyeballs out. He put on his red Boudin apron and a little beret ("Don't wear it like a baseball hat," Dawn said in passing. "It's a beret") and went to empty the waiting trays.

He was listlessly piling up trays on the top of the bin, when a man in a grass-green shirt, with a golfer-shade swinging a golf club in its coronary area said: "Young man, would you please come here!" Pronek obediently walked to the man's table and stood there, as vague hatred brewed in his muscles. The man had nicely combed blond hair, and Pronek could see the immaculate line disappearing into the pate. The man pointed at the croissant on his plate—there was a monstrous golden seal ring on his pinkie—and said: "I wanted romaine lettuce on my Turkey Dijon. Excuse me, but this is not romaine lettuce. This is iceberg lettuce. What do you have to say about that?"

Pronek was about to go and tell the sandwich person about the problem, but then, abruptly overwhelmed with a desire not to be there at the moment, said: "Nothing."

"I'd like my Turkey Dijon with romaine lettuce please," the man said.

"What's difference?" Pronek said.

"Excuse me," the man raised his voice, his double chin doubly corrugated in disbelief.

"Romaine lettuce, iceberg lettuce, what's difference?" Pronek said, with a sudden vision of stuffing the lettuce leaf into the man's mouth.

"May I talk to someone who can speak English, please?"

the man said and pushed his tray away with resolve, as the croissant shuddered and slid to the edge of the plate. Pronek felt pain climbing up his calves, passing his pelvis, to settle in his stomach as a cramp. He wanted to say something, something clever that would smash the man, but could not think of any English words that could convey the magnitude of the absurdity, other than: "Romaine lettuce, iceberg lettuce, what's difference?" He kept mumbling it to himself, like a magic word that would make him fly, and wobbled away in a vain hope that the man might just give it up.

But the man, naturally, did not give it up, for he demanded—and rightly so—full and responsible service for his hard-earned money.

Pronek kept cleaning the trays maniacally, filling up the bins with eviscerated bread-bowls, shriveled croissants, pizza edges, jagged watermelon slices, salad tidbits, slimy nonfat yogurt, jumbo-gumbo slough, filling up garbage bags, as if filling them up would stop the flow of time and stop Dawn from coming over to him with the man. As Dawn was walking toward him with the livid man in tow, Hemon looked at him askance, dragging a bag cadaver, as if trying to understand what might have possessed him to disobey. Pronek wanted to tell him, but Hemon, of course, would not have understood.

Thus, Pronek stood facing the man, as he ranted, pointing in the general direction of his croissant, while Dawn stood alternately looking at the tips of her blue shoes and glancing at Pronek, trying to place him as the main character of the man's story. When the man stopped his recitation, and looked at Dawn expecting her to come to the verdict, Pronek whimpered: "Romaine, iceberg, all same."

"I'm sorry," Dawn said. "But we have to let you go."

"I go," Pronek said. "No problem. I go."

Mind for Dummies

In the spring of 1993, Pronek found out, after a series of complicated information transactions—which involved a Red Cross person in Sarajevo, a ham-radio operator, a cousin residing in France, and Zbisiek, one of the Polish construction workers, who picked up the phone—that his parents were on the list for a convoy that would soon leave the city.

"When?" Pronek asked Zbisiek, whose blue eyes, framed by ruptured blood vessels, were moist with Slavic compassion.

"He didn't said it," Zbisiek said.

It was then that Pronek began fearing for his parents' lives, because—and this might sound strange to us—he realized that if they were killed they would not be able to get on the bus and leave the city, and, consequently, he would never see them again. He realized all of a sudden that people in Sarajevo were dying all the time, and that meant that whatever they wanted or needed to do next they wouldn't be able to do if they died: get up and walk in the dark, cold apartment; pee and then wash the dead toilet with a canful of water, previously used for washing their bodies; light a cigarette while hiding in the darkest corner, lest the patient sniper see the glimmer; sit down; cower; burst into tears; stand in a bread line, waiting for the soundless shell to land and kill. Before that, Pronek would feel for the people in Sarajevo he would see on TV, and the suffering was immense and well rendered. They had seemed capable of coming to the end of suffering, just like all the other suffering people, but death meant even the end of suffering. So he would watch CNN footage of people with familiar faces crawling in their own blood, begging the unflinching camera for help; people twitching and throttling as their stumps spurted blood; people who were trying to help them dropping like an imploded building, shot by a sniper; and he would know that was the end of their lives—that they would never touch a doorknob; never have their toes hurting in uncomfortable shoes; never flush a toilet; wear a condom; eat lettuce; suffer. Pronek realized that he had never known what death was and that he was never entirely present in his own life, because he thought—without really thinking—that it would last forever. He never thought enough of other people—his parents, for instance—because he never thought that they might die.

He looked up the word in the dictionary: *"Death*—the complete and irreversible cessation of life in an organism or part of an organism."

He remembered how his mother used to whine about unfolding his sticky, soggy socks before dropping them in the washing machine, and it hurt to know that if she never got on the convoy, he would never be able to tell her he was sorry now.

He began devouring Snickers and Babe Ruths and Cheerios and Doritos and burritos and everything he could put into his mouth, as if it were his ultimate morsel, so he gained thirty flabby pounds.

So long, handsome youth.

He worked as a busboy in a Mexican restaurant, until he dropped a pitcher of sky-blue margaritas into the lap of the local cop weighing some three hundred pounds.

He panicked, walking down the street, upon realizing that he didn't know the names of the trees (maple, chestnut, lime, oak, etc.) and flowers (marigold, petunia, lily, iris, etc.) and cars (Toyota, Nissan, Cadillac, Infiniti, etc.), and they all appeared as blank spots, like pages out of a photo album from which all the pictures had been ripped out. He forced himself to divert his hollow gaze from the streets he didn't comprehend, and walked looking before his feet: concrete cracks, flat cigarette butts, broken twigs, petrified footprints. He wished he were blind.

He enjoyed a series of interminable sinus infections, which produced a host of splitting headaches and stuffed his ears with thick earwax, whereby all the sounds around him were transformed into a continuous shushing hum, while he himself started mumbling. He couldn't understand anything people were saying to him, as he murmured incomprehensibly back at them. Accordingly, he started mumbling to himself, giggling, grimacing, and growling in response to his own inaudible discourse.

He had an interview for the position of a busboy in a Vietnamese restaurant, while the interviewer—a puny bespectacled man, armed with a cellular phone sheathed on his hip—looked at him, vexed.

He slept surrounded by paint cans, in the midst of a noxious mist. He would have to take the ladder out so he could lay the mattress down (the bed was gone), since the Poles had begun taking his room apart. The Poles clearly thought he had lost his mind, and one day gave him thirty-three dollars they had collected among themselves. Pronek muttered a thank-you in some super-Slavic language.

He stopped killing cockroaches, after he came back from an aimless walk and found the roach motel packed. He picked it up, yesterday's dried-up roaches hanging from the ceiling, and today's roach, stuck in sweet-smelling glue, turned its antennas toward him, greeting him. "Honey," Pronek said. "I'm home."

He began hating the blithe meaninglessness of baseball.

He worked as a parking assistant in the vicinity of Wrigley

Field, waving at cars on ball-game days, in order to mesmerize them into parking. He quit the job upon a painful epiphany of his absurdity, as he revolved his arm like a windmill.

He began thinking of himself as someone else—a cartoon character, a dog, a detective, a madman—and began fantasizing about abandoning his body altogether and becoming nothing, switching it off like the TV.

He couldn't watch movies in which people were killed and blown away with ease, because he began reconstructing the process of creating the blood-spurting effects and the movies became transparent.

He began hating Bill Clinton—spitting at the TV screen every time he was on—because he was able to produce a twinkle in his eye whenever he appeared before cameras.

He attempted to earn his crust of bread as a bilingual water-filter and health-inducing-cookware salesmen, which folded up after his supervisor-to-be—an ex-football player in a double-breasted suit and a goatee framing his fat, optimistic snout—told him that if he wasn't "gonna smile more and with more heart," there was "no buck in this business" for him.

He stopped desiring women, and began masturbating detachedly, not even fantasizing. Afterward he would spend hours in the shower, wanting to wash the filth off his skin, until he thought of water shortages in Sarajevo.

He began hating himself, because he was selfish, whatever he happened to be doing, just by being alive.

He stank all the time—even the inside of his nostrils stank—and people went around him on the street, and avoided sitting by him on the EL.

He answered a job ad, and listened to a voice saying, before he could say a thing: "Do you wanna make money?" "Well, it depends . . ." he responded, and the voice said: "This ain't no job for sissies," and hung up.

He began fantasizing about punching rock stars in their big fucking mouths, because they complained all the fucking time about being fucking unhappy.

We wish he had approached us then, we would have helped him.

He realized that his previous life was completely beyond anyone's reach and that he could entirely reinvent it, create a legend, like a spy.

He had dreams involving his parents: his father would sacrifice a rook in a chess game, and Pronek would beg him not to do so, for it would lead to a checkmate; his mother would take books off the shelves, rip the pages with pictures and then burn them in an iron stove, because she was cold all the time.

He interviewed for a job as a bike messenger, which was going marvelously, until he was informed that he needed his own bike and helmet.

He realized that he was invisible, and he desired being watched—he imagined a camera that would always follow him everywhere and record all the inconsequential and infinitesimal actions of his life.

He briefly worked the graveyard shift at White Castle, stealing the small burgers and taking them home to eat them cold, his pockets reeking of rotting processed meat and dissolving minced onion.

In the fall of 1993, Andrea's father came, struggling his way through the Polish debris, and solemnly informed Pronek that he would have to move out, for the apartment was successfully sold to a distinguished realtor, and they had to finish it as soon as possible—the Poles were to work day and night. Pronek saw the quartet of Poles shrugging their shoulders benevolently behind Andrea's father's back, and, numb with despair, announced that he was presently jobless, albeit looking for work. Whereupon Andrea's father offered to help him find employment in his wife's house-cleaning agency, known as "Home Clean Home."

Oh, what a lucky break for our immigrant.

Pronek took part in a delightful interview with Andrea's mother. "I know you're a hard worker," she said. "It is people like you who built this great country for us." She patted him on the back with the tips of her fingers and sent him off to the agency supervisor, a man labeled Stephen Rhee by the name tag on his heart. He was an ex-Marine, he grimly informed Pronek, and there was no screwing around with him. He had a crew cut, an immaculately ironed short-sleeve shirt, a bushy mole on his cheek, which looked like a tiny bullet wound from afar, and a tattooed eagle holding a rifle on his forearm. He tended to have a toothpick in his mouth at all times, and when Pronek told him that he used to be a writer, Rhee informed him that Jack Kerouac was the greatest writer of all time. "Dust is our mortal enemy, vacuum cleaners are our M16," he announced to Pronek, while showing him his locker, reeking of someone else's sweat. Before sending the crews out in the morning, he would install his fists on his hips and give a speech:

"I got four words for you: cleanliness, loyalty, shiny surfaces, privacy. We have to leave the house clean, 'cause this is a cleaning service, darn it. We work like a team, okay—if this guy leaves the bathroom filthy, then the work of that gal in the kitchen is all screwed up. Whatever is supposed to be shiny in that house must make you freakin' blind. And—get this into your empty heads—we are entering the temples of other people's lives. Don't you even begin to think about touching anything that does not need to be cleaned. There must be no traces of your being there, other than absolute cleanliness."

Yep, they cleaned in Hinsdale, Orland Park, Deerfield, Highland Park, Glencoe, Schaumburg, Oak Park, Wilmette, Winnetka, Forest Park, Lake Forest, Park Forest, Kildeer, Lake Bluff, all over Chicagoland.

Once they even went for a big job in Normal.

Being a novice, Pronek became a bathroom cleaner, "the shit boy." He would enter the bathroom and scan it first. He would look behind a shower curtain: the wall tiles smudged with soap and skin-froth; curled hair at the bottom of the bath-tub, like earthworms who didn't make it to the soft ground; the shower looming over the tub like a buzzard head; caged sham-poos, hanging on the shower's thin neck. The toilet gaping, the seat lifted and the bowl specked with urine droplets; pubic hairs stuck to its side, as if climbing up; a crumpled and soiled piece of toilet paper behind. The mirror dotted with tooth-paste foam, sprinkled from someone's mouth last night; tooth-paste tubes writhing below the mirror, with a thumbprint in the middle; liquid-soap bottles, like limbless flamingoes, with the nozzles sticking out; stolid bottles of beauty: moisturizers, replenishing creams, aftershaves, conditioners.

Upon inspection, Pronek would clean, slowly and merci-lessly effacing all remnants and traces of bodies. He grew to like doing it, because he would stop thinking about himself and everyone else, focusing on hairs and stains, enjoying their steady, inevitable disappearing. The whole world would be re-duced to a pimple-pus speck on the mirror, which he would swiftly wipe off. Everything in the bathroom would attain mind-absorbing magnitude, and he would become smaller and smaller, until he would completely abandon all thoughts of himself and everything outside that bathroom and become a transcendental cleaning force. Having finished cleaning, he would feel purified, as if his self changed profoundly while being away from him.

In that manner, he became a true professional. His wage rose from $6 per hour to $6.50 per hour, and Rhee allowed him to go occasionally on "solo missions"—cleaning Lincoln Park or Gold Coast condos alone.

Oh boy, did he like that: entering the apartment and the owner's scent—perfume, shower gel, shampoo, deodorant— still lingering; furniture summoned around the TV, with a couple of proud dressers backed against the wall; maps of the world, ochre (which meant old), with dragons dipping in the corners; Ansel Adams's photos of vapid gray desert valleys; small colorful carpets stretching on the floors like lazy, content cats; a tall CD rack, the Sears Tower of the condo; a staunch bookshelf with books standing straight like soldiers at atten-tion: *Independence Day; Seven Spiritual Laws of Growth; What's Inside—A User's Guide to the Soul; The Client; The Heart of Darkness; Eating in Tuscany; Investing Today; Mind for Dummies; Theodore Roosevelt: A Life; The Alienist,* etc.; flower pots hanging from the ceiling like miniature gardens of Babylon; an array of family pictures on the piano gazing slightly upward, like afternoon sunflowers; a bowl full of trin-kets: pennies, marbles, matchboxes, business cards, condoms, paper clips; a wine rack with black bottles, like a hearse; a sign on the wall saying "No Parking—Tow Zone"; a softball tro-phy, with a golden figure on a tiny pedestal throwing a golden marble ("Grace Cup '92"); the computer and its black screen closely monitoring his every move.

Sometimes, Pronek would sit in a comfortable armchair, and try to imagine his life in this condo: he would walk in through that door, still checking the mail—stacks of letters from his friends, from all parts of the world—take off his shoes and wiggle his toes. He would go to that tall, handsome bottle of scotch and pour himself a generous drink, sip, and let the warmth slowly coat his bowels; he would check the messages ("Hi! Ahmm . . . this is Grace, returning your call . . . Ahm . . . I'll be real busy next week, but I think I can squeeze you in next Friday . . . Ummm . . . I kinda like Italian food, I guess . . ."). He would go, still sipping his drink, to the closet, slide the mirror, and hang up the navy-blue jacket, shirts, and suits hiding coyly behind each other's backs, still happy to see him. And in the morning he would turn on the radio ("Inbound Dan Ryan pretty packed . . . Outbound Kennedy moving smoothly . . ."). He would fry a couple of eggs in the Teflon pan, while brushing his teeth, spitting the foam into his kitchen sink. He would have parties on weekends, invite his friends, and then, afterward, after the last drunken guest had left, he would make love to Grace—a voluptuous blonde from White Pigeon, Michigan—on the sofa (because they were too horny to make it to the bedroom), watched by a chorus of martini glasses, some of them violated by a cigarette butt. Sometimes, when truly blue, he would dim the lights, open a bottle of Chardonnay, play some blues (*I'd Rather Go Blind Than See You Walk Away from Me*), and get slowly drunk, until he passed out.

Having cleaned the condo, he would then go back to his apartment—a hollow, furnitureless studio, looking at the El tracks, which he had recently rented for $285—lie on the floor mattress, watch the ceiling fan revolving above like a gigantic demented dragonfly. Pronek understood that to maintain the sameness of every day the fan had to keep revolving; he had to leave for work at the same time, and come back with the same train; his lunch always had to be the same baloney with Wonder bread. As long as every day was as any other day, his parents would be alive, still waiting to get on the convoy.

As we're charting the foreign territory of Pronek's mind—expanding westward, as it were—we must not omit the marshes of involuntary memories he mired in for a while.

The first one overwhelmed him abruptly, as he was gorging himself on farmer cheese mixed with sour cream, with green onions and rye bread. As soon as the medley of tastes—the cool milkiness of farmer cheese, the pungent, sneezeful greenness of green onions, the sweetness of bread crumbs scratching his tongue—reached the palate, a shudder ran through him. A billow of warm sorrow invaded his senses, a feeling isolated, detached, with no suggestion of its origin. He took the second morsel, chewed it sluggishly and—as the mulch slid down his throat—a memory raised slowly, like leavening dough: a summer afternoon, late July, in Sarajevo, on their balcony, looking westward at the sun setting behind the squareness of the building with big, red letters on it reading: "Long live Tito"; he was reading a comic book ("Tarzan vs. Interpol"), dropping moist chunks on the pages (Tarzan fighting a villain on the Eiffel Tower); his father reading obituaries in the back of the paper, sighing pensively, paper rustling; his mother watering flowers, their turquoise trumpets twinkling around the edges in the counterlight, niggled by bees; a bunch of his loud friends (Vampire, Cober, Deba, Armin) shouting from the park under the balcony: "Pronek, come down, bring the ball out. Let's play cowboys and Indians!"; the sun crawling behind the "Long live Tito" building, and all the shades on the balcony disappearing from the concrete exuding warmth, until the night blanket covered everything.

Thus began a period of some twelve months in which Pronek was perpetually dazed, for the involuntary-memory sensations were no longer routine perceptions, but rather an unpleasant burden, which forced him to wallow dolefully in his previous life.

He would enter an apartment to be cleaned, and walk into a cloud of fragrance (Magie Noir) left by an absent woman, and he would instantly recall burying his face in Zu's hair, the tickling silkiness on his cheeks; he would clean the bathtub and the chlorine stench of the cleaning potion would bring back cleaning squat toilets in the army, his hands burning afterward, the steel ball of nostalgia grinding his bowels; the smell of burned grease in the kitchen, as he was scrubbing the stove, followed him through Bascarsija, where kebab shops spewed barbecue smoke, and the uneven stone pavement under his feet made him wobble; the dust aroused by the vacuum reminded him of Saturday mornings, the cleaning time in their home, when his mother would make him crawl under the bed to reach the clusters of dust backed up against the wall—he would lie there, enjoying seclusion, his cheek stuck to the cold parquet, until his mother's stodgy feet appeared by the bed; a sun-smudge quavering on the wall above the piano was the same one as the one on the inside of the tent wall, as he drowsed tranquilized by the heat, the tent full of the cheap coconut smell of sunscreen; pencil shavings in the basket by the desk had the same pungent, wooden smell as the color pencils he shared with Mirza, his best friend in elementary school, bringing back the September scent of waxed floors and wet chalk boards and clean children's clothes; an array of books on the desk—three of them spread like pinned butterflies, pressing against the desk surface, their spines sticking out, as if they were doing push-ups—was on his desk once upon a time.

His head became bigger and heavier; his spine was slowly curling into a question mark; and he walked—when he walked at all—bent forward, his gaze fastened to his toes, like a dummy slowly deflating.

A Rose for Pronek

But while we were up to our waists in Pronek's stream of consciousness, dear reader, fly-fishing for the psyche, the world did not stop revolving, the clock did not stop ticking. For three years have inconspicuously passed, and we're sprouting back into the spring of 1996. In the meantime, Pronek's parents never got on the convoy; Pronek's father was wounded by a sniper; the TV screen became saturated, oversaturated, undersaturated, and then the exactly-opposite-of-saturated with images from Bosnia: several more broadcast massacres in the city; the mauling and massacre of Srebrenica; some more Western muscle flashing; friends shot by snipers or killed by shrapnel; rape camps; starvation stories; burning villages; Karadzic, Mladic, Milosevic shaking hands with someone; the end of the siege of Sarajevo and the war; talking to his parents once a month or so. Pronek went through all this in an aching daze, never—we're proud to say—underperforming at his work. In fact, he became a single-condo specialist, developing a healthy herd of steady customers, who never saw him but regularly left tips for him under the fruit bowl, or on the coffee table. Now he was able to save up some money and rent a one-bedroom apartment in West Rogers Park. The apartment had slanted floors; door posts askew; hissing, hysterical silver radiators; an ancient, pink, four-legged bathtub; and an army of medium-sized cockroaches, clearly comfortable, if not excited, to have him in the apartment. We're able to submit a telling image from the first night he spent alone in the apartment:

Pronek on the floor, sandwiched between two thin, gentle blankets, the floor pleasurably hard; he's looking across the room, the freshly polished floor glistening, like the lake on a moonlit bonanza night; in the opposite corners, miles away, in the dimness of otherness, his two suitcases, like Don Quixote and Sancho Panza—the thin, tall suitcase full of books and papers, and the fat one bulging with dirty clothes and a couple of soggy towels.

In the morning, he would wake up in pain, and proud of it. He would sit on the only chair and eat cereal and milk out of a leaking wooden bowl between his knees (he hadn't had enough to buy a table), and watch a morning sunbeam coyly entering his apartment, like a curious squirrel. Oh, the nippy mornings of the 1996 spring. The warm winds peeled off the snow cover, but there were still decaying snow patches around, like spit-foam. As he was riding somnolent buses down Devon on his way to the El that would take him to work, his past nightmares transmogrified into the haze of the morning present. He watched the street gliding by, looking for signs that he was awake and, indeed, alive: a revolving breasted bust in the wedding-dress store window; Beanie Babies piled up in Noah's Ark; women in saris walking down Mozart Street; World Shoes; East-West Appliances; Universal Distributors; a man in a white shirt installing a bucketful of roses in front of his flower shop; Cosmos Press; Garden of Eden Cocktail Bar; leaflets taped to light posts, signposts, mailboxes reading "Pray for wisdom for Mike"; Miracle Medical Center; Acme Vacuum; a tailor-on-duty sign held by a tailor dummy. Every morning was like the first morning, because Pronek would forget the morning at the end of the working day.

One morning in April, Pronek saw, through the mizzly curtain, the tailor dummy waving at him. He decided to go to

Sarajevo, because he realized it was all right, because the incredible thing was that every place had a name, and everybody and everything in that place had a name, and you could never be nowhere, because there was something everywhere. The only way, Pronek thought, to be nowhere was not to be at all.

How is this related to his decision, we cannot fathom.

In any case, he saved up a little more money, bought a plane ticket, and flew to Sarajevo, via Vienna, in May. Presently, we will give him his voice back and let him talk for himself. Ideally, of course, he would speak in his native language, but, unfortunately, that is not possible. Here are, then, his authentic, fresh, and realistic experiences:

As the plane was descending, I saw ochre patches, like scars, in the greenness of the mountains.

The houses along the runway were bullet-ridden, and as the plane was touching down, I felt as if I were inside of a bullet speeding toward the target.

I gave my passport to the man behind the glass pane. He looked at the passport, then he looked at me, then he looked at the passport. Behind his back, there was a young man in a dusk-blue suit and a tie as thin as a wicker. He had a cellular phone, and glanced around, monitoring the arriving passengers. Then he leaned over the uniformed man's shoulder, glanced at my passport, then at me. He was a spook.

Dobrinja, across from the airport, looked like it was marauded by a world of ravenous termites. It looked built of holes and about to crumble. There was yellow tape stretching everywhere, reading "Mines."

The cab driver did not turn on the taxi meter and I suggested he should do it. He said, with a gorgeous mumbling Sarajevo accent, What are you worried about? You'll pay. But how will I know the amount, I asked. You'll know, you'll know, he said. We argued, until he pulled over, turned toward me, unbuttoned his shirt to show me a scar near his navel and said, Listen, I didn't spend four years in the trenches, defending this city, to turn on the taxi meter now, all right? All right.

Building after building pockmarked with bullet holes, gouged out windows and lives that used to go on in those apartments, piles of rubble, burnt cars, burnt buses, burnt kiosks, burnt streetcars. This is the movie theater where I saw Apocalypse Now *for the first time, burnt.*

As soon as I stepped out of the cab, I saw Aida. I hadn't seen her for years. When we were kids, she drew a heart on her forearm and inscribed my name on it, with a ballpoint pen. I was happy to see her, I hugged her. She was married, she had a son, born in the middle of the siege. I was so happy to see her. How is life? I said. How is your mother? Her mother used to make heavenly baklava. Her mother was killed, she said, by a sniper, at the beginning. She saw it, because her mother ran ahead of her across a sniper-watched street, she was struck and killed instantly.

My mother and my father were waiting in front of our apartment building. My father embraced me, and we stayed locked, saying nothing. Then my mother embraced me, and she wept and wept.

A bullet had hit my father in the left cheek and then had simply gone out the other side. He had two scars on his cheeks, like two symmetrical warts, and he lisped now. He said, Had I had my mouth shut,

*I would've been dead. The Kalashnikov bullet is very light, he ex-
plained, but has a high velocity so when it gets inside the body and hits
the bone, it doesn't stop, it ricochets around, tearing everything apart.
See, he said, if the bullet hit my teeth before it went out, it would have
bounced around all over my head, shredding my brains, until my head
was all mushy inside, like a watermelon.*

*I went through my parents' apartment, touching everything: the
clean, striped tablecloth; the radio, with seven ivory-colored buttons
and a Donald Duck sticker; the grinning African masks; the carpets
with intricate, yet familiar, geometric patterns, full of gashes, from
under which the parquet was gone, burnt in the rusty iron stove in the
corner; the demitasse, the coffee grinder, the spoons; Father's suits,
damp, with shrapnel slashes; the black doorknobs, the cuckoo clock, now
defunct; the crystal vase, the complete works of Joseph Conrad, half of
which were gone, burned in the stove; the dripping faucets; the pictures,
black-and-white and color. There's the three of us on the beach in
Makarska, my mother on the left with a scarf and dark sunglasses, my
father on the right with a cigarette dangling from his mouth, me in the
middle, sitting on a confounded, sad donkey with a sombrero on its
head.*

*There were no windows in the room that used to be mine. Instead,
there were nylon sheets, with UNHCR written on them, in blue, orderly letters, flapping and bloating in the wind.*

*I went out for a walk with my mother. My father didn't like to go
out anymore, except for work, because he always felt that someone was
watching him. She showed me where Vera, their neighbor, was killed.
As soon as Mother and Vera stepped out of the building, arm in arm,
Vera was hit in the heart and swirled to the right, my mother showed*

me the pirouette, and she just dropped right here, still clutching her
purse, and then she throttled, spewing blood. I didn't know what to do,
my mother said.

On the pavement, all over the city there were roses—the points of
the shell impact. A tiny crate and a few straight lines, of uneven
length, like sun rays on a child's drawing.

There was a rose of the shell that massacred the bread line on
Ferhadija. Amela, a friend's daughter, died there. A piece of shrapnel
entered through the back of her head and burst out through her face,
taking it apart. Adil, her father, operated on her himself, putting her
face together, so they could bury her properly.

There was graffiti on the wall by "Egypt": "Samir loves D." Who
was D? Where would she be now?

I looked at Trebevic, a peaceful mountain now, dark and silent.
My father pointed at it. The Chetniks could see us like the palm of
their hand, he said. Right above the roof line, he showed me, was the
front line, a thin gray thread in the green, barely discernible.

I thought I would never see you again, Veba said. He lost about
thirty pounds. There was not much to eat, you know. Rice or nothing,
he said. I had to climb up to the fifteenth floor to get to his apartment.
The next door apartment was hollow, charred black, pigeons nesting
and cooing. Veba spent the war in the Bosnian army, but now he
wanted to go to Canada.

Veba said he worked with a guy who used to be a sharpshooter and
was kind of famous for killing two girls on the other side with a single

bullet. He was on the top of Hotel Bristol and they were playing somewhere across the river.

There was the intersection where I had the only car accident of my life, rear-ending a tractor. The streetlights were out, one of them was dangling like a shot-off limb, right above a scorched ambulance car.

My mother and I finally talked my father into taking a walk with us. Neighbors greeted us, and we greeted them, and sometimes we would stop and talk. And how is America? they'd ask. Fine, I'd say, hard work. We walked by the Miljacka, under the blooming crowns of chestnut trees. The river had been the front line, so the trees had not been cut for firewood. We walked to the apartment where I used to live. Some refugees from eastern Bosnia lived there. Nice people, my parents said, but very scared. They would let you in, probably, to look around, but they would be scared.

We stood across the street, looking at the UNHCR nylon. A shadow passed across the nylon screen, then another one. I could imagine them preparing a meager dinner, going over to the cupboard, taking out plates, setting them up on the table. Then taking out the utensils, dropping a fork on the floor, perhaps, then spitting on it and wiping it with a cuff. I could see them sweeping and washing the floors; washing the tub; scraping the filthy film in the sink; scrubbing the toilet bowl; vacuuming the carpets. I suddenly had a feeling that I had stepped out of my life and that I was watching myself, that the shadow behind the nylon was me.

I imagined standing in a water line, surrounded by plastic vessels, and then a shell comes soundlessly out of nowhere and hits the asphalt

and the person in front of me is mowed down instantly. I can sense that
something is wrong with my body and I look down and I am kneeling,
my thighs are ripped apart, spouting blood. I topple over and bang my
head against the pavement, but there is no pain, I am surprised. And
right in the line of my rapidly fainting gaze there is the rose, still
warm, filled up with the blood oozing out of my head. But I could
never imagine the moment of death, I could never imagine vanishing,
so my imagination stays fixed on the rose.

Mozartkugeln

"There is no way you can get in," the Austrian officer said,
tightening his pale lips to express the disapproval of Pronek's
attempt to enter Austria without a visa. The width of his mustache exactly matched the width of his mouth at that moment.
Pronek stared into the officer's greenish eyes, clutching his
Bosnian passport in his extended hand. "But all I want is to
take look at Vienna," Pronek said. "I'll be right back. I won't
stay. I am alien resident of United States."

At that moment, Pronek understood that he was an oxy-
moron.

An Asian man, with his shoeless feet propped up on his
suitcase, leaning back on the seat, watched the interlocution
with drab disinterest. Pronek looked at him as if he were to be
a crown witness of supreme injustice, but the man just averted
his eyes and looked at a wall-wide ad picturing the Alps,
promising clean water, clear air, healthy heights, far from
stinky alien crowds.

Pronek went up the escalator, with his handbag full of
clean knitted socks and bourek, devised by his mother, and
stopped to stare at the door, revolving counterclockwise, con-

templating an attempt to get out, until he saw steel bars preventing that possibility.

"Passenger Katzelmacher, please report to the Information desk," a willowy electronic voice from above said.

He went uphill, tired people stretching uncomfortably on blue seats along the wall. He saw a Bosnian family with recognizably flat, square heads. They were lumped together, probably convinced that separating for a moment would put them in danger of never seeing one another again. A mound of a man, his navel peering out, with a flat briefcase on his rotund belly, ascending and descending. An African child in a Liverpool jersey, bundled in his mother's lap, looking out, his eyelids slowly sliding down, closing. A man reading Russian newspapers, his brown-socked feet parallel on top of his shoes. There was a tie store, with millions of pendant ties, with only slight variations in pattern and color, dementedly echoing one another. A group of Americans led by a woman clad in an American-flag dress, her wide butt star-spangled, strolled by with their hands full of duty-free shopping bags, laughing vociferously. He saw one of the Americans, a tall, blond man, dropping his Redskins hat, not noticing and walking away, and Pronek felt a twang of glee. He imagined spending his life here in the transit zone of the Vienna airport, pickpocketing for a living, robbing Americans blind every time a planeload of American optimism and resolve was delivered. He wandered into a store populated with Mozarts staring at him askance from the box-tops. All of them had their lips tightened into a narrow line and seemed to be worried about something.

Pronek bought a box of Mozartkugeln, though he could think of no one to give it to.

"Passenger Katzelmacher, please approach the Information desk."

Pronek approached a camera store. There was a little screen in the window and he recognized himself on the screen. He looked up and saw a tiny camera above the entrance, like a motionless, black hummingbird. He waved at himself, and he waved back at himself. Two veiled women walked into the store and began examining a Polaroid camera. He decided not to enter the store and went to the Johann Strauss Café. He crossed his legs and watched the departure billboard, and all of a sudden a tsunami of changes went through it, and Moscow was carried from the top, on the crest of a rapid wave, to the middle, where it settled down right above Bangkok. A waiter, balancing a weighty tray on three fingers, flitted by, and then began unloading plates, putting them in front of a man in a black shirt unbuttoned to his navel, and silver cross dangling between his nipples. The waiter finally put down a humongous mug of beer, and the man guzzled down half of it, before the waiter stepped away. Then he wiped the froth from his upper lip and looked straight into Pronek's eyes.

Pronek asked for a glass of mineral water, cold.

There were people sitting in a circle, with their backs to a marble pile from which water patiently oozed. A man with a black wide-brimmed hat frowned, smoking and dropping the ashes into the palm of his left hand. A man in a tweed jacket with suede elbow patches and a gray, academic beard, flipped through a *Penthouse* with a woman named Grace breasting on the cover. A stream of people poured through one of the rectangular metal detectors, as if they had materialized all of a sudden, beamed down from a distant planet. They all spoke a language Pronek could not locate, occasionally clapping hands in front of each other's faces. A woman pushed a cart with a little girl on its prow, like an admiral.

"Passenger Pronek, please report to gate number one."

Pronek left the carefully counted Austrian coins at the table, drank the mineral water to the bottom and sauntered over to the duty-free shop. Johnny Walker, Winston, Jack Daniels, Milde Sorte, Jim Beam, Captain Morgan, Rothmans, Smirnoff, Davidoff, Coco Chanel, Jean Paul Gaultier, Absolut. Pronek walked out and looked at the departure billboard: Moscow was at the bottom, about to be gone, and he had three more hours before the flight. He did not want to fly to Chicago. He imagined walking from Vienna to the Atlantic Ocean, and then hopping on a slow trans-Atlantic steamer. It would take a month to get across the ocean, and he would be on the sea, land and borders nowhere to be found. Then he would see the Statue of Liberty and walk slowly to Chicago, stopping wherever he wished, talking to people, telling them stories about far-off lands, where people ate honey and pickles, where no one put ice in the water, where pigeons nested in pantries.

But, of course, they would never let him out of the Vienna airport, and he had to get to work on Monday.

"Do not leave your baggage unattended!" the voice warbled.

Pronek roamed back to the Johann Strauss Café and saw the man with the silver cross, guzzling down another mug. On the plate in front of him there were two identical, parallel, crescent bratwurst, along with two symmetrical puddles of ketchup and gall-yellow mustard. He felt ravenous hunger. He sat down, summoned the waiter, and ordered the bratwurst. There were violins pinned to the wall, above the Mozart-full shelf, like wingless butterflies. A gray-haired man was squeezing by between the tables, his arms and face splattered with shingles. Pronek realized that the man in the black shirt had a ripening boil on his neck—a fiery red bulb protruding right above the collar. Pronek called the waiter, labeled Johann, and informed him that he had changed his mind and he didn't want the bratwurst. The waiter glared at him, curling up his upper lip, his apple cheeks fidgeting, and then coughed a little, perilously close to retching, saying nothing. He pulled out his pen, glaring around, and his little order-taking pad, and scratched Pronek away.

"Passenger Pronek, please report immediately to gate number one," the willowy voice said, with a tinge of anger in it this time. Pronek finally recognized that it was his name that was being called and ceased peeling the Mozartfoil, the Mozartglobe already peering out suggesting pleasures, but he questioned the reliability of his perception, and discarded the call as another instance of aural hallucination.

"Passenger Pronek, please report immediately to gate number one!"

Now this time Pronek could not deny it. He looked around and noticed everyone staring at him with expectation. He bit into the Mozartball, picked up his hand baggage, and commenced walking cautiously toward gate number one.

We could see his reluctance, his clumsy, indecisive gait, and his crumpled, stained shorts, and his green ten-year-old corrugated polyester shirt. He walked toward the gray rectangle of the metal detector warily, as if aware that once through the gate there would be no way back.

He munched the other half of the Mozartkugeln and rolled the foil into a little ball. He stopped and looked around, as if waiting for a signal, or the audience applauding. Then he looked toward us, but he couldn't see us behind the gate. We were waiting, knowing that he had nowhere else to go. But he showed no desire to get over there. He made a couple of wobbly steps and then stopped, unwrapped another Mozartglobe, bit into it, and just stood before the gate, chewing and smiling at us, as if he knew we were there.

IMITATION OF LIFE

For a long time I used to go to bed early, but then my parents finally bought their first TV set. I remember full well crouching behind a gray armchair, in the corner of our living room, hiding from the images of a creature that had three legs, a long snakish neck, and a fist-like head, with a furious only single eye sending lethal rays down on terrified people and buildings. The buildings looked like weak, grotesque matchboxes, compared to the progressing monster blowing them, with its gaze, into flaming dust and smithereens. I hid behind the armchair, but—every once in a while—I'd dare to look at the TV across the room, the fake furry texture of the armchair rubbing my cheek, and the horrors on the screen would send me, with bellows, back behind the chair. I would lie down on my convulsing belly, trying to be as tiny as possible, the geometrical, colorful patterns on the carpet as close to me as the inside of my eyelids. I do not know what my parents did while I was writhing in fear, but I remember being alone—there was no one and nothing between me and the three-legged destroyer, apart from the armchair. It had awkward plywood armrests and stubborn, eternally creaking, springs. The movie being shown was, I'm inclined to believe, *The War of the Worlds.*

When I was sick, I would lie in the living room, because of the TV, and watch *Sesame Street* or *Survival.* There would be a little chair by my wrinkled bed, an ex-sofa, with an array of bottles, pillboxes, and lozenges, and a mountain of blown-through and crumpled paper napkins. My mother would pull down the green shades and I would sometimes disregard the TV and, benumbed by a persistent fever, do nothing but watch a sunbeam, which would manage to squeeze in between the two shades, move across the room, pointing, like a blind man's cane, at things unawares.

And it would stumble upon a bad reproduction of an irrelevant Soviet painting, picturing a desolate autumn forest path. The beam would start on the left side of the painting and go over the stunned cluster of dun and gray birch trees, as if counting them, turning them ochre for a long moment. Then it would go over the assembly of souvenirs, brought by my father from Zaire, on the fake-ebony chest: an erect elephant tusk, pointing at a dark wooden mask with a mouth strained into a gaping grin; a baked-clay owl, enameled in carmine, orange and lemon-yellow colors, with bulging eyes that would follow me all over the room. I would fade in and out of languid, confusing dreams and the beam would move quickly, as if crossing a dangerous street, across the opposite wall. I would look up and, above my head, in the sunbeam, a stream of specks would flow upward, like air bubbles let go by a diver. Then it would go over the heavily laden bookshelf, over the stiff spines of my father's Russian math books, unperturbed by their intricate titles, and it would finally stop at the right end, and, depending on the season, insist on a spine-torn *Beekeeping Encyclopaedia* or a never read, orderly lined-up, pristine *Selected Works of Joseph Conrad*. After that, the beam would cautiously retreat, toward the cleft between the shades, and then it would vanish. The room would fill up with, first, turquoise, then, maroon dusk. The night would set in and the things in the room would become immobile, obscure, silent, and I would lie, listening to the encroaching hum of darkness and my own wheezing slowly disappearing in it.

A thing not to be forgotten: a radio, model "Universal," with a plywood shell that would reverberate and tremble when I'd turn up the volume to the last notch. The upper front part was covered with burlap-like cloth, behind which one could discern the circular shadows, like breasts under a shirt, of the two speakers. At the front bottom there was a narrow ledge with buttons—like an accordion keyboard, except there were only seven buttons. When the far left button was pressed, the light would go on behind the screen with the names of all the cities of the world: Abu Dhabi, Edinburgh, Cologne, Ankara, Baghdad, Warsaw, Barcelona, Dresden, Cairo, Athens, Copenhagen, Moscow, Vladivostok, Córdoba, Dacca, Dakar, Djibouti, Andorra, The Hague, etc. The right knob controlled the volume, the left knob made the red line between the light and the screen slide behind the city names. Sundry languages would turn into static cracking, bleating, and wailing, or a bass hum, and then back into a different language. I would stop the red line behind a city name—say, Munich—and then listen to the incomprehensible language. I would picture the people who were talking—only their heads, in fact, for I couldn't imagine their bodies. I would imagine a round-faced, bearded man speaking in Moscow, smacking his lips after every successful sentence; a pale, blond woman warbling from Monaco; an angry, teeth-clenched man in Lagos. Sometimes I would try to guess what they were talking about. I could tell when they were reading the news, because of the flat dullness of their voices; when they were praying, because of the submerged pain in the sounds they were making; when they were reading poetry, because of the whining and undulating. But sometimes they would just speak and I knew nothing about what they were saying: were they talking about their own lives? about their children? about their history? were they telling stories? about what? These meaningless voices were somehow mesmerizing, like music, and I could imagine the space, the streets and buildings and rooms behind them. I could hear the curling, passionate streets of Rome: gurgling Vespas and people at the market arguing over the prices of tomatoes. I could hear the gray sternness of the Potsdam voice: cubic, symmetrical buildings with wide, spacious streets where people looked minuscule and stifled, and policemen stood at corners with leashed German shepherds. I could hear the clamor of the great city behind the Cairo voice: everybody on the streets, the voice passing through a narrow street full of haggard people in burlap robes, selling heaped fruit and strange pastry, and there's a cage hanging over the door, nearly walled off by shelves burdened with fish, and in the cage there's a dog, a small, anxious dog, with big flappy ears, and its curious eyes are burning with a red glow.

One day, I fretfully unscrewed the plywood from the back of the radio and saw the heated, dusty lamps, still, positioned according to some unfathomable logic, like chess pieces. I stared at the entrails of the radio, inhaling warm sneezeful dust, and I didn't know how it all worked. There were entangled colored sinews connecting the lamps: some lamps had inside a thin glaring wire, like a trapeze, and some of them were dark, as if whoever was in there was sleeping.

My best and only friend's nickname was Vampire, because he had long and conspicuous eyeteeth, and when I was seven his mother died. She was a tiny, skinny woman who did little but smoke and gossip. Then she abruptly shrank and then she died. "Cancer!" they told me. After the funeral, I had to go to their apartment, they said, just briefly, to pay my respects. I walked into a boxy room full of whimpering adults in black. Someone shoved a glass full of warm, but colorful—flaming orange and red—liquid into my hands. Everyone seemed to have a burnt-to-the-filter cigarette between their blistery fingers. They reeked of sleeplessness, misery, and warm, stale beer. Men were unshaven, with black sleeves rolled wearily halfway up their forearms. Women wore black sweat-soaked scarves around their sallow faces, dabbing tears and sweat-pearls above their lips with the scarves' corners. They scurried around, mindfully serving people who would reluctantly enter the room, as if stepping into thick, retarding mud. The clock on the wall, with an immobile pendulum, showed 12:02, and the hands were palsied—the second-hand had stopped between five and ten. The mourners told me the clock was stopped at the exact moment of her death and that it would never run again, as long as they live. I sat there, uncomfortable, with burning armpits, for some time, listening to them morosely retelling stories about her life: how she made the best potato soup ever; how she wanted to listen to the weather forecast the Monday she died, and that week was to be sunny and delightful; how she fell asleep on a streetcar and went around the city with it for hours, finally getting off at the wrong stop, not knowing where she ended up. Then I downed my turbid drink and left, sheepishly saying: "Goodbye," to everyone, which no one really noticed, except for a young woman who carried a plateful of chicken thighs, and who, in passing, pinched my ruddy cheek with her greasy fingers.

The playground was in the center of the park, square, surrounded by the bushes, and in the middle—a square within a square—there was a sandbox. There were also a slide and a merry-go-round, a couple of swings and seesaws, and six benches at the edges, all rusty and shabby, positioned randomly, like mountains. The playground used to be covered with fine gravel, which was thinning out now, and one could see patches of black dust with glass shards, here, and there, glittering meekly like lit, distant windows. The sandbox used to contain fine beach sand, but most of it was gone and the sandbox was full of gravel and black dust, just like everything else. We would run around, Vampire and I, chasing each other, or playing soccer, or simply fighting, and there would be a fog of dust around us, sticking to our sweaty skin and tongues. Our throats would be dry and scratchy and we would clear them, producing a harsh, choking sound, and then spit. The spit would hit the ground and roll in the dust, like a gelatin marble, and then it would stop, as if exhausted, and sag, drying into nothingness, coated with dust. Sometimes, we would ignore the seesaw, slide, and swings and climb a large lime tree at the edge of the park. We would clamber to the top and then look at the other children as though they were at the bottom of the sea and we were in a boat, fishing.

The cinema was called Arena and I didn't know what that word meant. It was freshly built, so it was clean and all the colors were strong—or is it that I just remember it clearly and that these days no color is sharp or bright. In any case, I can easily picture the spring-green doors, with strawberry-red handles and locks, and the breathing, cold, attractive, crepuscular darkness gaping behind. In the display box, on the left of the doors, there was the poster of the film being shown, usually rather old. I'm able—with some effort—to remember the poster for *Imitation of Life*. There was the story of the movie: "When a young actress (Lana Turner) meets a young photographer (John Gavin) she cannot know that he will be the love of her life. But when she chooses her career over her love for him she cannot know, alas, that she's making the greatest mistake of her life, etc." Alongside the story, there were retouched, cumbersomely sumptuous, colored stills: Lana Turner on the beach, her eyes sky-blue, her hair golden, her teeth snow white, her skin virgin pink, and behind her a painted crowd, thousands of blissful bland Americans, none of them discernible from the mass; Lana Turner facing John Gavin, who is holding her shoulders, as if trying to lift her off the field of silky verdure and save her from sinking into it.

We were perched in the crown of the lime tree, enjoying our elevated invisibility—we could see girls on the swings and an old man dozing off on the bench while trying to read. A rivulet of saliva would occasionally trickle down his chin, he would wake up with a sudden grunt and look around in a slight panic, as if embarrassed by his dream, or afraid that everything might have disappeared while he was asleep.

A dog trotted into the park and stopped by the sandbox. It looked at the swinging girls and then it looked at the old man. We clambered hastily down the tree and rushed toward the dog. It scurried away, retreating a bit, stopped and looked at us.

His pinkish-brown tongue hung out of his mouth, like a dead squirrel. He looked as if a dun rug was thrown over his scaffold-skeleton. He had a straight cicatrice line on his hind thigh, as though he had been lashed with a belt or a chain. There were beige patches of skin on his neck and ass, and his tail was cut off. But he stared at us and would not go away, rearranging his gaze every time we moved toward him.

In the summer, I would sit on the balcony facing west, the tips of the top branches of a maple tree fluttering and obscuring children playing in the park. I could only hear their voices and see them intermittently running between branches. They would use terrible, vile words and I felt guilty for eavesdropping, but I couldn't stop. Feeble cloudlets of cigarette smoke would rise, like sighs, from the balcony below and would mingle with the scent of blooming lime trees, warm concrete and dust, stirred up by children in the park. I'd sit there and watch everything throb with being, and listen to the hodgepodge of noises. Often, I would see an old man, wearing an aging pair of sandals and a straw hat, walking higgledy-piggledy across the street, throwing his arms around, shoulders leaping, as if he were exploding in a series of unstoppable hiccups, twitching his head back, and forth, making one step forward, and then one step back. It would take him a long time to get from the corner of our street to the entrance of his building. I would see his face, flashes of cramps and helpless grins, as if he was perpetually surprised by pain—I knew he couldn't help it—always on the verge of falling down. I would watch him and his long hobbling journey home, and I wondered why that was happening to him and not to me. Years later, I would learn he had a debilitating disease that breaks down old people, but he was long gone by then, having left just a memory of his stubborn straw hat, which would never fall off his quaking head. I would only sometimes see his wife—an obese, tired woman— walking a black poodle, which would stop now and then, oblivious to the limp leash, and, after some retching, cough out a clot of brownish sludge.

The whole school was going to the cinema and, while we were impatiently waiting to cross the street, a lean girl with long, pony-tailed and dark hair, much older than any of us, ran across the street and, after a deafening squeal, was hit by a polished red Volkswagen. She went up like a bouncing ball, levitated for a blink of our flabbergasted eyes, and then she went down, with a whump. There was a moment of silence and then a boy in a navy-blue jacket started screaming. We were rushed away and, a little later, walking two by two, holding each other's trembling hands, sang a song our teacher ordered us to sing: "With Comrade Tito, the people's fearless son, not even hell will stop us . . ." In the cinema, we saw *Snow White and the Seven Dwarves,* and I could hear the boy sobbing the whole time.

On our way back, everything was normal at the street crossing—the girl and the car were gone. Except, close to the pavement, among balls of dirt and black motor-oil puddles, there was a sneaker, bright blue, with the sole face up and a piece of pinkish chewing-gum stuck to the heel. When I was returning home from school, it was raining. The sneaker was still there, and a rainbowy rivulet, descending from one of the oil puddles, went cautiously around it.

So we ran, Vampire and I, to our respective homes and brought back the needed nourishment: boiled eggs, chicken heads, a bottle of milk and, also, one of the beaten enameled pots that Vampire's mother (he said) used to use to make potato soup. We watched the dog lapping up milk, while he raised his languid gaze every once in a while and looked at us, as though trying to recognize us. But he never would and he would just delve back into the milky pot. Vampire wanted to name him Tito, but I thought we could get arrested for that, so we named him Sorge, after a spy I had read about and wanted to be like.

Once in a while, I'd sneak into the cinema, when the bored usher wasn't watching. Or I'd ask an adult to claim me as his (or her) child and take me in without paying the ticket. I sat in the front row, next to a complete stranger, feeling safe in the darkness, my head tilted back. Before the show, there'd be a smiling woman on the screen, always the same one, with sparkling eyes and a beehive hairdo, looking and pointing at us, asking us not to smoke, so we never did. The screen was vast and concave, as if preparing to envelop us. The close-ups were gigantic: once I realized in horror that I could fit into Clint Eastwood's mouth, like a cigar. I could see the texture of the image overlapping with the texture of the screen. Right above my head there was a long, floating whirlpool of dust inside the fat, barely conical beam of light. The newly sprayed hay-fragrant air freshener struggled to overwhelm the sweat, cheap aftershave, and perfume brought from the outside. The chilling darkness of the cinema would glide over my skin, making me intensely aware of the boundary between the world and me. Sometimes I'd be so cold I shivered, but it was impossible to leave. I'd sit in my seat, freezing, about to pee in my pants, my thighs glued to the seat-skin, until the very end of the credits, reading all those unpronounceable names piously and wondering who were those people. Why were their names important? What did they do? Where were they? Were they alive?

Vampire managed to convince me that the mistletoe berries growing on the lime tree were not only delicious, but also capable of making me immortal and endowing me with incomprehensible power. After I had eaten several berries and then began retching, Vampire, in a moment of malicious inspiration, ran to my door, rang the bell, and told my father what I had done, omitting his role in the incident. When I got home, my father told me, with grave sincerity, that the mistletoe berries were deadly poisonous and that I should expect to be dead within a day. What could I do?—I trusted him. I burst into moribund tears, for I'd been promised to be taken to see *Battle of Neretva* the coming Saturday. I asked my father to spend my last hours with me. He lay on the bed, and I pulled down the shades, turned off the TV, deleting the quiz show he had been watching. I lay by his side, my head on his vast chest, I could hear his sonorous heartbeat, like a clock. I inhaled the scent of his Pitralon aftershave and waited to die, staring patiently into the darkness. I could hear an excited radio voice, coming from someone else's apartment, whinnying in delight, for someone, somewhere, had scored a long-awaited goal.

In the building across the street, on the first floor, there lived an old woman named Emilija. Her face was being dragged down her skull like a glacier, wrinkles echoing one another, and the skin on her thin, fragile arms hung down, like dough. I thought she must have been beautiful when she was young. She always had formerly white gloves on her hands and a colorless scarf wrapped around her head, like a turban, but that was only because she believed that her neighbors wanted to overwhelm and suffocate her with dust, which they somehow kept blowing through her walls. The blinds on her windows were perennially closed and, at night, I'd see a flimsy shadow, projected on the blinds by a single source of feeble light. I'd see a silhouette throwing up her long puppet arms and pointing and shaking a finger at something or somebody beyond the screen window. Sometimes, she'd abruptly open her window and shout in a piercing, exhausted voice: "You want me to go away, but I shall not! Not ever! Go to hell! You want me to suffocate! Let me tell you! I can't die! I'll never die just to spite you! Go to hell!" Once, in the middle of the night, she threw out a bottle of milk, shrieking: "Poison! Poison!" The bottle shattered on the pavement and the milk puddle, awkwardly shaped, like a sea on a map, scintillated back at the street lights.

We built Sorge a house out of a sturdy cardboard box. We put cushy towels on the cardboard floor and even an embroidered pillow, which Vampire stole from his home, while his father was away drinking. Sorge would follow us everywhere. He'd sit in front of the cinema exit doors, as we exalted over the adventures of Shaft or Agent X. He'd doze under one of the park benches, as we oscillated on the swings. When it was time to go home, we'd have to keep him busy, if we wanted to sneak out on him, with bones and eggs. He was stinky and filthy and was populated by a colony of fleas, so, one day, after a sudden rain had washed him, I stole some money from my mother's wallet and bought a can of bug spray—with a picture of a cockroach writhing in unspeakable horror under the triangular shadow spreading from the picture of the bug-spray can. So we sprayed Sorge. Vampire held him around the neck, as though hugging him, and Sorge stood patiently, stamping his hind legs a little, like a horse being groomed. I sprayed him all over, particularly the patches. When Vampire let him go, Sorge dutifully licked his face and sauntered away and then lay down under the slide.

And then the nonsmoking lady would reappear, with the same unperturbable smile, and I would exit the cinema with a stream of people trickling into the blazing day. I was blinded every time. I'd close my eyes and stellar spots would glide across the inside of my eyelids. Everything was deafening: bleating car horns, the fractious rumble of the traffic, the clamor and shouts of children playing soccer, radios turned on everywhere. I'd open my eyes and the world would be back: square, concrete, gray, and cacophonic, far from the mesmerizing tranquillity of the screen and darkness. I'd wish to have not seen the movie, so I could see it again and go through the same unforgettable deluge of sensations, but I'd immediately know I couldn't—for time always went only forward, as in films. I'd know I could never go back and prevent losing a precious moment, and a warm wave of painful sorrow would keep spreading through my body, until it would moisten and blur my gaze.

We found Sorge in his house petrified, lying sideways, his legs stretched out stiff, his jaw taut in a horrible grin, gums pale, eyes wide and lackluster in terrified surprise. We tried to push him and wake him up with a wooden stick, but the stick quickly broke. We dug a shallow hole behind the slide and buried him there. We put the potato-soup pot on the grave, lest we forget his gravesite, but the next day the pot was nowhere to be found.

My father was gone when I woke up, and I thought I had died. I didn't know if I was still the same person or someone else, so I didn't dare move. I tried to hear or sense my pulsating heart, but everything was mute. There was a diligent beam of light coming through an obscure hole in the shades and I saw busy motes of dust levitating in midair. I heard someone shouting: "And you can go fuck yourself!" and a remote slamming of a door. The radio was still on, but the ecstatic voice was not there, just shrill gibberish. It was dark and cool, I was hungry and I had to pee. I looked at the clock on the wall, dimly gleaming, but I couldn't see the hands moving. I got up, doubtful, opened the door and found myself facing a torrent of light, in the midst of which my father was listlessly watching the quiz show. "Welcome back!" he said.

When I finished the first grade with mild success, my parents bought me a watch as a reward. It was circular, with large slender numbers rounded up and a convex glass above them. The second-hand moved in tiny jerks and I could never catch the moves of the bigger hands, although I would stare intently. I looked at the watch often, fascinated with the immutable tenacity with which the needly hand vaulted over the stolid numbers. I would touch my pulse and look at the watch and the steady synchronicity of the two rhythms soothed me. I had to wind my watch every night before going to bed, I was told, lest it stop while I was asleep.

After a night of unsettling dreams, I woke up and saw two Nazi flags through my window: red, with white circles, like eyes, and swastika-pupils, flapping on the train station. They taught us that the enemy never slept and I thought that it had all come back. I ran toward the train station, bumping into a woman—her hands full of bags loaded with lean green onions and chubby peppers—who didn't seem to be disturbed in the least by the flags. There was a field of injured German soldiers, lying on the rail tracks, with bandaged heads, arms, and legs, with stains, here and there, of crimson blood. Some of them were standing up, smoking and laughing. One prostrate soldier, with a large blot of blood on his chest, leapt from the stretcher and ran, chortling, toward a group of soldiers sitting in a freight train car with a red cross painted on it, their booted feet dangling cheerfully. I elbowed my way through the forest of legs belonging to the throng of calm civilians, and got to the front row. There were two German officers walking down the train station corridor and then opening a door and entering the building. Above their heads, there were hanged rugged men and women, revolving on thick ropes. One of them smiled at me, revolved once, winked, went through another revolution, and smiled again, shrugging his shoulders. The two German officers again walked down the corridor decisively, with black-steel machine guns, firmly grasped, pendant around their necks. They opened the door and got in. Then they got out, went back to the end of the corridor, turned back, waited for a moment, and walked back, determined, their mouths tight shut, uniforms neat, black glistening boots sternly brushing away dust and pebbles. They opened the door and got in. Then I saw the camera, moving sideways in front of the crowd, toward me, on narrow, thin rails. When the officers opened the door the camera would stop and then go back to the end of the rails and wait for the officers. The crowd stood there, with its hands in its pockets, soundless and motionless, just a throng of eyes following the officers, hypnotized. Then the officers stopped walking down the corridor, lit, with relief, their cigarettes and sat at the threshold of the door. The crowd was dispersed and the camera taken off the tripod and moved elsewhere. They took down the hanged man above my head, he twisted his head, first left, then right, stretched his arms, as if imitating an ascending airplane, and then dissolved into the mass.

ACKNOWLEDGMENTS

Operation Bruno would not have been possible without the support and patience of my wife, Lisa Stodder, the toughest editor around and an important intelligence source, who was able to handle all my shifting identities with grace.

Agent Nicole Aragi, the head of the New York network, and Sean McDonald have been instrumental in completing the New York part of the Operation.

The Chicago operatives Reg Gibbons and Stuart Dybek generously put their trust in me. The Chicago part of the Operation would have been impossible without the murky character of Edwin Rozic (known in some circles as Eddie the Neck) and the Herman Lavoyer Special Soccer Unit. Particular thanks to George Jurynec and the Ukie boys for providing a safe house in times of adversity.

The Sarajevo operatives, scattered around the world on their dangerous missions, have unconditionally believed in the success of Operation Bruno, putting their well-being and sanity on the line. My being would be impossible—let alone Bruno—without Gusa and Veba. The group of Sarajevo operatives trained in Omladinski Program and Dani, particularly Zrinka, Pedja, Zoka, Senad, Herr Wagner, Drug Tito, and Gazda Boro Kontic (the man behind it all), have performed miracles of misinformation and propaganda. The wisdom of Semezdin Mehmedinovic has provided moral and mental guidance for a young literary-field operative.

Finally, the nomadic Hemon tribe protected me in times of adversity, as my parents, Peter and Andja, and my sister Kristina (still fighting international criminals), provided honey, pierogy, and love, which sustained me during Operation Bruno.